FREEDOM'S LIGHT:
The Letitia Carson Story Begins

Janet F. Meranda

Illustrated by:

Anna Austin

October, 2016

TABLE OF CONTENTS

Preface

By the time Keizer Community Library planned a talk by Jane Kirkpatrick, I was already an avid fan of Jane's books. I was also intent on having her write a novel about an amazing pioneer African American Oregonian, Letitia Carson. I had discovered her through my research partner during our graduate class in historic archaeology at Oregon State University in the 1980s. While Jane was autographing my collection of 10 of her 25 books that evening, I gave her a two-page proposal for a new story, and the rest as the cliché says "is history."

A Light in the Wilderness, which chronicles the life of Letitia Carson in Missouri, her trip over the Oregon Trail in 1845, and her life in the Soap Creek area of western Oregon, was published in 2014 following two years of research discussions, writing, editing, and re-writing. The first edition sold the highest number of copies in the first month of any of Jane's books and sold out in just a few months, won the WILLA Literary Award and was nominated for the Spur Award. Then it was the first of Jane's books to be translated into Dutch and published in Europe. In addition, the German edition has just come out in 2016.

I wanted Jane to write another book to tell the rest of Letitia's story. While I was asking her to work on a sequel, Jane was encouraging me to consider writing a prequel instead. *Freedom's Light* is my first novel; it explores history and life in early American slavery in Kentucky for Letitia and her mother up to the point where Jane's novel picks up the decision to leave for Missouri. I am so pleased to have Letitia's story in the public eye, to be a part of this project, to have met and become friends with Letitia's descendants. I'm looking forward to working with Jane on her next project.

This book is intended to be not just an enjoyable read but also a resource to assist middle school and young adult students in understanding the conflicts and challenges for early slaves brought into the United States.

The cover photo is Martha Carson Lavadour Carpenter, daughter of Letitia Carson, born on the Oregon Trail in 1845. The photo was provided by one of her great grandsons, Joey Lavadour of Pendleton, Oregon.

Janet Meranda

Keizer, Oregon

Major Characters

Titilayo/Martha	Letitia's mother, Bowman slave
Ayoke/Letitia	Martha's daughter, Bowman slave
Binta	Martha's housemate, Bowman slave
Callie	Letitia's best friend, daughter of Polly, Bowman slave
Henry	Martha's "husband," Letitia's father, Barnes slave
Abraham and Margaret Bowman	Kentucky slave owners
William and Sarah Bowman	Son of Abraham and Margaret
Hiram and Millicent Barnes	Bowman family neighbors
David and Rebecca Prinzlau	Bowman family neighbors

Prologue

Don José Barbosa, being a typical ship's captain from the royal Castilian area of Spain, cared not a whit what the British said or wanted. He was short, thin, olive-skinned and overbearingly arrogant in his fancy clothing, pencil-thin mustache, and sharply trimmed goatee. He fully intended to continue sailing his ship, the *Feloz* (Beloved), to Brazil and the Caribbean islands. So long as he exercised due caution, he expected to either outrun or outgun any opposition that came across his bow. The *Feloz* sported 16 large cannon which were a deadly combination with the professional skills of his gunners and absolutely assured their safety on the high seas. The sugar-rum-slave trade triangle had been functioning like a well-oiled machine for nearly two hundred years, and would, no doubt in his mind, continue to, in spite of the prohibition against slaving ships passed by the British in 1807 and the Americans in 1808.

The *Feloz*, loaded with multitudes of sparkling beads, bolts of bright cloth, sheets of shiny copper, a few ancient muskets, and a huge supply of rum in large oak casks, had sailed to the coast of West Africa in the Spring, her captain planning to be safely home again ahead of the hurricane season in Jamaica, which would begin in June. Captain Barbosa's crew of 46 experienced sailors, one slave overseer, and two cabin boys, who had just turned 13 and were on their first voyage, had spent the past month doing ship repairs. Buckets of fresh tar were smeared on the joints, replacement sails were sewn and the galley restocked, but their favorite time was spent drinking rum on a beach on the inner passage opposite Sherbro Island in Sierra Leone. Barbosa kept well out of sight of Freetown, which lay just north of Yawri Bay, while bargaining for captives brought from the interior. Neither he nor his men had any desire to deal with that large settlement of ex-slaves who would certainly take a dim view of their business. The men were more than happy to rest, relax, and enjoy the company that arrived every few days to entertain them each night while they waited to load the newly acquired cargo and start the long, dangerous trip northwest to the New World.

By dividing the space into three-foot high layers between the quickly cleared cargo decks of the *Feloz*, Barbosa now had room for at least 500 slaves as well as his superb crew. He knew of ships that allowed only 18 inches for each layer of shelves, but he hated to waste space on slaves who would surely die in such circumstances. Yes, 1809 would be a highly profitable year so long as he kept his head clear and held firm to his plan. The Fula might be smelly, and now very drunk, savages, but they never failed to find good merchandise – strong men and shapely women – to trade for cheap bits of this and that and, of course, many cups of rum. This last group to arrive had been more

Sierra Leone. Sherbro is the large island off the southwest coast. Freetown is situated on the central coast next to an estuary north of Yawri Bay. See Map Appendix, Page 166.

than satisfactory, with very few younger children, who were the least likely to survive and who brought the tiniest prices. He considered them carefully and decided they could recuperate on the ship. He rechecked his cargo log for the final count of 526 slaves, 321 males and 205 females. It was time to get everyone organized to head west.

"Francisco," he called out. "Timeo. Get the crew rounded up and let's get started. We have a lot of work to do if we're going to leave on the morning tide."

Captain José Barbosa

Chapter 1

Going, Going, Gone

Titilayo huddled in misery on the sand, the earlier flood of tears now dried on her almost charcoal-colored cheeks. At only 12 years old, she was still short with the slim, almost boyish figure of a young girl just moving into womanhood. She had been taken, along with her mother Teniola, from Shaki located just slightly southwest of the Oya (or Niger) River during a midnight raid. Her father Oriri had died trying to protect them and the babies from the nomadic Fula who happily scavenged slaves from any village or hunting party they could overwhelm. He was left crumpled on the ground within the circle of burning homes next to the bodies of her younger sister, youngest brother, and 10 other toddlers and babies who couldn't walk to the coast.

Titi's mother, though just having come from the isolation of the maternity hut, had been her marching partner for the first several days as they headed due west toward the headwaters of the Niger and then to the coast beyond. Until, that is, she collapsed and was beaten to death because she could not rise again. The 25 in their single chain of women and girls walked behind the first of the three long chains of men and boys who had been clubbed into submission and locked together. The women being within sight of the men and under the constant threat of a cat o' nine tails, allowed no offer of rebellion.

West Africa Rivers. The Fula took their prisoners west toward the Niger River headwaters and on to the coast where they could be sold. See Map Appendix, page 165.

Once they arrived at the coast, each captive received a fancy ℬ brand on his or her chest. The ostentatious iron, designed by Captain Barbosa himself, lay in the fire on the beach, ready day or night to reinforce his ownership rights. Titilayo noticed that some of the lighter skinned captives had multiple brand marks on their bodies, showing that they had been slaves even before being brought to this deserted coastline and sold to these unusual strangers.

11

Ade and Mba had remained silent during this torture as befitted their status as young warriors, but Titi knew her older brothers were suffering from fever and chills. Would they live to once again be her guardians? The men sat as close together as possible, doing their best to keep the boys safe and warm within the circle. If it had been allowed they would have surrounded the women and girls too, but that was strictly forbidden. The men and older boys all felt terrible shame for this failure on their part. At first they had tried to reassure the young people but every word brought an immediate and violent reaction from the strangers. So, they slowly gave up trying to speak and settled for smiling at the girls whenever they could catch someone's attention. Titi had heard her brothers more than once so she knew they were staying strong.

Everyone knew the rumors of what would happen to them once the entire load of people was crammed into the ship that rode gently on the waves just off the coast. The strange, pale men with hairy faces would take the ship far out onto the great water and nobody would ever be seen again. It had been said in horrified whispers that the pale ones even ate the littlest children they captured, although Titi had seen none of this so far.

Tears once again welled up in Titilayo's eyes. She no longer had her mother to help her acquire the skills she needed to become a marriageable woman. She had learned how to farm the land beside her, but who would teach her to butcher and cook an antelope, or thatch a roof, or weave the reeds in big sections for house walls? She could make indigo dye and create a simple garment for herself but how would she clothe a husband? Where would she find one so far from home? In one night her world had come undone, shattered beyond recognition.

She had no idea where she was going. She had no hope. She fell into a restless sleep as she prayed that the spirits would let her die soon, at least before one of the strangers decided to take her for himself.

A man's loud voice startled her awake. What was happening? The strangers were running about, shouting and striking at their captives, dragging them to their feet in the waning light, and shoving each chain toward the collection of the smaller boats which were scattered at the water's edge. This couldn't be good.

Chapter 2

The High Seas

In fact, Titilayo couldn't see how it could be any worse. The first night on the ship, anchored in the bay, caused many to be sick and the smell just contributed to more serious vomiting. Early the next morning, just after daybreak, the anchor was raised and the ship turned to face the unknown sea. Day after day, chained to one another in the dark, unable to move unless everyone did so at the same time. Many were weak from lack of wholesome food, constant nausea as the ship rolled its way along, and daily abuse. The continuous odor of vomit and feces was nearly overpowering. They tried to encourage one another with forbidden words of comfort, but despair was rampant. They took turns crying out to the men on the top deck, begging to be released for some fresh air and a cup of water but the only response was the face of a man peering through the barred hatches, his harsh voice shouting -- for silence or threatening a whipping – in a language they couldn't understand.

One night Titilayo heard Mba's quiet voice in the dark hold; he was singing a hunting song. They were not her words to sing, but she hummed along under her breath. Slowly the other men of Shaki took it up:

"Come brother eland, you are needed.
Come brother duiker, this man is hungry.
Come brother gazelle, before this day is done.
Come to me now, that your death may be painless.
I honor my brothers for their gifts to me."

There was great sorrow in the repetitive music; would they ever hunt again? Yet, Titi understood their desire for unity and the bonding of the age cohorts. They had learned trapping and hunting skills as a group of young boys and hunted together for years. First for hyrax, pikas, and shrews, then for monkeys and bats; they were proud to contribute to the stew pot. Finally they took their places with the men ranging out to search for the herd animals that would feed whole families.

The voices fell silent when they heard the grate being removed over their heads and a heavy body clumped down the ladder. They hated this time above all others. Night after night, one chain of women was taken away. Their cries and screams could be heard to the lowest level causing the men to curse and wrench at their shackles until their ankles bled. There was nothing they could do when the women returned with eyes swollen shut and blood running down their legs. Titi had been forced to take her own turn with the sailors above. The first time had been a horror beyond thought. Now she cried silent, bitter tears but she had stopped struggling; it didn't do any good and just earned her another beating.

15

After weeks of sickness, torture, and death both below and above deck, the pale ones instituted a new routine. One chain at a time was unlocked and hauled up to the deck for a bowl of corn meal mush every morning. Buckets of sea water were thrown over their heads to rinse away the filth and help heal the lash marks and pressure sores on backs and legs. Nobody knew exactly how many had died and been thrown overboard to the delight of the trailing sharks; they had given up counting once the tally went over both hands and both feet of the man who had been keeping track. However, it was clear their captors didn't want to lose any more cargo if they could help it. Those few minutes of freedom made the holds much more difficult to tolerate and their small breakfast was frequently surrendered to the refuse piling up on the floor.

In another week one of the rigging sailors called out and all of them began jumping about, whooping and shouting with glee. Titilayo was fairly certain this couldn't be good. Although, she had to admit, it was a relief when the ship stopped its incessant rolling. Strange voices could be heard from outside, even an occasional familiar word. What was happening now? More fearfully whispered rumors raced from one end of the ship to the other. At daybreak the hatches were unlocked and thrown open. Even though it was early in the day, intensely hot sunlight streaming onto the bodies in the hold brought tears to many eyes.

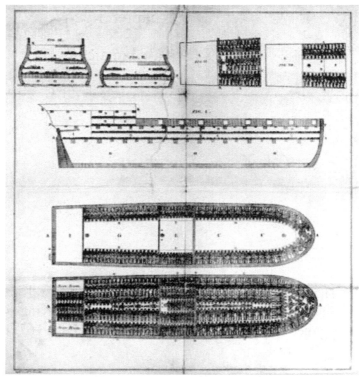

"The Men, Women and Children were crammed into every available space. There was no room for people to move, eat or breathe. There was a great smell due to the people's faeces.

"An example of a slave ship used is the 'Feloz'. The Captain José Barbosa recalls: 'She had taken in, on the coast of Africa, 336 males and 226 females, making in all 562, and had been out seventeen days, during which she had thrown overboard 55. The slaves were all enclosed under grated hatchways between decks. The space was so low that they sat between each other's legs and [were] stowed so close together that there was no possibility of their lying down or at all changing their position by night or day.'"

Chapter 3

Sunny Jamaica

The island of Jamaica is 51 miles wide and 146 miles long. Savanna-la-Mar is on the southwest coast. Kingston is on the southeast coast. See the Map Appendix, Page 167.

Each chain was taken up separately. The captives were stunned to see land and people with dark faces amongst the pale ones. The sailors called it Jamaica and hurriedly doused each captive with fresh sea water and scrubbed them with a brush. Then most of the men and a few of the women were led down a wooden board and off toward the market place in the town of Savanna-la-Mar. Savanna lay on the coast at the southwest end of the island. The women watched over the ship's rail. Where were her brothers going? Why was she being kept behind? Bewildered, Titilayo watched and wondered until they were out of sight. She hoped with all her heart that they would come marching back again soon.   Many of the women wailed piteously for husbands and sons, but it did no good.

"E n le. Nibo ni o ti wa? Ki ni oruko re?" Ade called out to the Yoruban standing on the dock, "Hello. Where are you from? What is your name?" Others of the captives spoke to different people. None answered their greetings nor their polite inquiries though skin tones, body shapes, hair styles, height or lack thereof, and distinctive scarification patterns made their tribal affiliations obvious to any observant eyes. What was wrong with them? The man with the whip waved it under their noses and they figured they were being commanded to cease talking to their fellow countrymen who walked with heads down and eyes averted behind various light-skinned residents of the town.

In the shed at the market, each man was neatly oiled and taken up on a platform before a horde of staring faces crushed into the space below. There was much shouting between the stranger who seemed to be in charge and the browned but still pale faces in the crowd. The men were ashamed to have strangers poking and prodding their bodies in even the most private places. And women in the crowd stared avidly at their naked bodies; it wasn't right. Nobody was sure exactly what was happening, but the captives were being led away, one or two or a few at a time. Once an entire chain went together. Captain Barbosa had stepped into the crowd to speak with a tall younger man with sun-bleached blond hair who was dressed in a white linen suit and mopping at his heat-reddened cheeks with a cotton handkerchief.

"Senor Thistlewood! Tomas! I am honored that you have come to view my humble offering this fine day." The Captain waved a casual hand at the group of men collected at the back of the platform. "What kind of purchase are you looking to make? Will this be for yourself or are you bidding on behalf of one of your patrons?"

"Ah, Captain Barbosa," the young man exclaimed while removing his hat and offering a sketchy bow. "I thank you for your gracious greeting. Today I buy for myself and you know I will be most interested in young, strong, healthy men and older boys. I don't want to waste my time and money on any who are old, fractious, or infirm. Besides working on my own farm I will want to be able to rent them out during the sugar cane harvest. Do you have a good selection that I might consider?"

"Certainly, Senor. I will instruct Hernandez to bring out my best for you." The captain stalked over to the auctioneer, pulled him aside, and hurriedly explained the special request. For a virtually guaranteed sale, he

Jamaica Sugar Cane Harvest.

was more than willing to be accommodating. Savanna had proved to be as good a market as Kingston with far less crowding and danger.

Barbosa watched the proceedings with hawkish intensity and seemed much pleased when Thomas offered £40 each for the 10 older teenage boys who had weathered the voyage in the best condition. Most of the rest of the cargo being offered for sale here were the biggest, strongest troublemakers and he was well rid of them at almost any price. The overseers at the major sugar cane plantations would keep them under tight control or kill them. Who cared? He would have his money, and he would deliver the best of his cargo to an even better market.

Yes indeed, this would be his most profitable voyage yet. If he could keep up the pace, maybe he would think about retiring to Gibraltar or Cadiz on the Spanish south coast in a few years. The thought of lounging in the warm Mediterranean sun, sipping fine wine, and chatting with friends brought a small contented smile to his stern face. His black eyes gleamed with pleasure at the thought.

Maybe he should consider Jamaica instead. There were some very nice estates here. Either way, it would make his wife happy and keep her out of his business if he decided to move his mistress too. Or maybe he should start looking for a younger, prettier replacement. No matter. Life was good!

Montpelier Estates St James, from "A Picturesque Tour of the Island of Jamaica," oil on canvas painted by James Hakewill, 1820-21. Copyright expired. See http://www.wikigallery.org

The sailors would stand guard over the remaining cargo for the few days they stayed in port. They would take turns shoveling out the hold and scrubbing the boards of the filth. From now on the captives would have more room to sit and sleep, chamber pots to keep the floors clean, and fresh food every day. Their good health was of supreme importance once they began the final leg of the trip to the previously English colonies.

He would give his men shore leave before continuing on to America. Mayhap he would even invite Mr. Thistlewood to join him for a drink at the Negril, a favorite watering-hole near the docks. It always paid to cultivate the men with plenty of cash money in their pockets. What was one more day, more or less? The Americans would still offer premium prices for his premium cargo.

The slaves, which included both of Titilayo's brothers, sold on the block in Savanna, joined half a million of their fellows. A few worked in shops and taverns in the town, but most lived in tiny huts and labored daily from dawn to sundown in the cane fields under the sharp-eyed scrutiny of overseers who wielded their whips with deadly accuracy. On Sundays they worked split half days so that the work was done but each also got a bit of extra rest. While the crops had to be tended, none of the plantation owners and/or overseers wanted to waste the investment they had in the workers. Of course, if one was an escape artist or a deadly physical threat, well then punishment could be anything up to and including death by whipping to set a good example to the others. It was accepted that it had to be done upon rare occasions. After all, one hated to waste one's hard-earned money.

Every day Titilayo used her deck time after breakfast to search the docks and what she could see of the streets beyond for any glimpse of Ade and Mba. Every day she was taken back below having seen nothing of any of the absent men from Shaki nor any of the other captives. What had happened? She just knew this wasn't good.

24

Chapter 4

North America

The *Feloz* left the port with a few less than 300 slaves to be sold in the new United States. Barbosa knew that the more beautiful women and less rebellious men would fetch high prices in the market at Wilmington on the Cape Fear River in North Carolina. Tobacco, rice, and indigo were major crops and cotton was just beginning to become an important export item in the southern states; all were extremely labor intensive. The men would no doubt go to the fields to fuel the booming economy of the South. The women would become cooks, maids, and mistresses on the larger plantations or in businesses in the towns. The *Feloz* crew members were looking forward to a larger than average payday when they arrived home in a couple of months. The remaining captives were more than depressed to leave behind family and friends to continue traveling to a land about which they knew absolutely nothing. Now Titilayo was sure that she would never see her brothers again.

* * * *

Barbosa brought the *Feloz* skittering safely past the Frying Pan Shoals and Bald Head Island before worming his way through the multitude of tiny islands in the river to the port docks at Wilmington. Thankfully there had been no sign of any American ships bent on interfering with his mission. Once the *Feloz* was safely tied up, the captives were cleaned, oiled, and dressed in cheap cotton garments to be presented to the eager buyers awaiting their first view of the new shipment.

North Carolina wasn't as hot as Jamaica, but it was every bit as humid. Not a face in Wilmington was dry; the sweat ran in miniature streams. Some of the residents held ever moving fans, while others sheltered under fine lacey parasols. Still others simply stood quietly and allowed their slaves to wave small leafy palm branches above their heads to evaporate some of the moisture and keep away the flies and other irritating insects.

The first few samples of merchandise stumbled their way to the platform as excited murmuring rustled through the crowd. The market for slaves had been steadily growing in the years since the colonies had finally thrown off the much detested British rule, and the bidding competition had also grown stiffer. The wealth of the South was displayed in its architecture, fashion, home goods, recreation, and every other aspect of life. Having more slaves just proved that one was worthy of the highest rung on the social ladder. Lace gloves covered dainty hands but each woman unhesitatingly whispered advice to her husband on which slave would best serve the needs of their household.

Titilayo took her turn on the block, doing so with head bowed and hands clasped over her abdomen. The auctioneer grabbed her chin and forced her head up so everyone could get a good look at her. He extolled her virtues in a loud voice – her youth, strength, agility, beauty, docile personality – anything and everything he could think of that might prompt increasingly higher bids. If he did a really good job, Captain Barbosa would slip him extra pay at the end of the sale and he intended to earn the largest possible bonus today.

An entire chain of teen girls and young women was purchased by a dealer who would take them inland to Louisville, Kentucky where more eager buyers would flock to its market. Titilayo would be among this group. She would join with the others walking along behind another new stranger wondering: Why was she here in this strange place? Where were they going and what would happen when they got there? She was alone and grief-stricken, but she determined in her heart to do whatever she could to live according to her people's laws and traditions – they might make her go here and there but they didn't own her spirit!

The guide moved slowly and stopped for meals on a regular basis in order to maintain good health in the slaves. It would take at least a week's worth of steady travel to arrive in Louisville. After conducting a quick sale in the market he could head home again to shop for more prize merchandise.

* * * *

"Pa, Pa," the sandy-haired teenager tugged frantically at the elbow of his father's shirt, "What about that one? She looks pretty young and healthy. Let's bid on her!" His freckles stood out in spite of the sun-burned redness of his cheeks. His mother would not be happy that he'd forgotten to take a hat when they left home in the pre-dawn darkness to make their way north to Louisville.

"Son, we don't have enough money to go after a prime piece of flesh like that; besides, we'd have to take time out to train her. We want an older woman who already has the skills we need for living up country. We'll wait a bit and see what else will do better." He shrugged off the teen's grip on his arm and moved closer to the young slave woman selling glasses of cold tea, under the watchful eye of her owner. He'd much rather have a beer or even a shot of bourbon, but beggars couldn't be choosers so he'd take what he could get. Besides, it would be a long day in town and he needed a clear head to find what he wanted at a price he was willing to pay.

The bidding was brisk, and Titilayo was purchased separately for $105 by a middle-aged fellow dressed in a good but wilted-looking tan linen suit, which fit him a bit snug around the waist, and wearing a light straw hat atop his balding head. Mrs. Barnes huddled close to her husband, whispering to him from behind her best summer fan. She hated the heat and humidity but couldn't pass up an opportunity to show off her new dress in a classier social circle. She loved the light yellow taffeta frock covered in dark yellow flowers, sporting short puffy sleeves, lace threaded with ribbon at the neck, and adorned with frills of lace near the hem. She'd been assured that it was the latest fashion from Paris. She kept a close eye on other women in the crowd trying to determine if they had noticed and appreciated her new gown and matching shoes.

"Look, Pa," the young man exclaimed. "Ole Mr. Barnes has bought that girl. What do you suppose he wants with her? He's a bit long in the tooth, don't ya think?"

"Hush now, William." His father scowled darkly at his oldest son. "What he's doing is none of our business. You look. Here comes a likely candidate for our farm. Pay attention now and learn what it takes to be a gentleman farmer."

Mrs. Barnes' Taffeta and Lace Gown.

Mrs. Barnes, smiling smugly, was pleased to be getting a young house slave that would learn to do everything she wanted in exactly the manner she wanted it done. The children needed a tight rein and she was just too tired to be chasing them all over creation, besides it wasn't lady-like.

She would keep this slave – hm-m-m what should she call her? Martha. Yes, a nice, plain name -- close by her side, out of reach of the men! Although, she speculated, just maybe she could pawn her husband off on this newcomer and avoid any more babies herself. It was something to think about, the idea could be considered carefully on the long ride home.

She looked forward to getting out of the lowlands of the Ohio River floodplain, even though the Kentucky hills weren't much cooler and society was certainly lacking in the graces. It was, however, her home and she was the queen of their little kingdom.

Chapter 5

Kentucky Hills

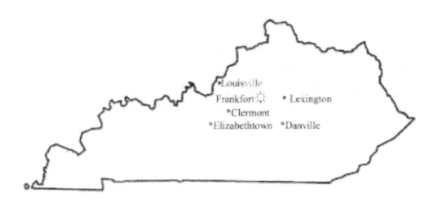

The Barnes-Bowman neighborhood in north central Kentucky. See detailed Kentucky map, Page 168.

Six months later, the queen was in a royal snit. "I'm telling you husband, Martha's either a halfwit or deliberately disobedient. I can't take any more of this. No matter how hard I try she doesn't seem to understand a thing I say. She can't sew a straight seam, has broken half my best dishes, lets the children run wild in the dirt; I have more work now than I did before she came. Do something before I have to be taken away to an asylum!" Her voice had risen with each breath she took. Her green eyes flashed with pent up anger and frustration as she stamped her foot at her chagrined husband.

"Now, now, my dear. What exactly am I supposed to do about her? She seems bright enough to me. And, she's gonna give us a bonus any minute. Good thing the auctioneer in Louisville didn't know or she'd have cost me a lot more. I want to get my money's worth, regardless. Maybe she just needs a firmer hand."

"Hiram, don't you dare blame me for her stupidity. I want you to see if you can trade her off to the Bowman family up the road. See if they'll give up their house slave or at least one of their smarter field hands. Offer them whatever it takes to get me a girl with a brain and don't waste any time. I tell you I'm going crazy!"

It was obvious to poor Mr. Barnes that he really had no choice but to acquiesce to his wife's wishes. She would just pester him endlessly until he followed her instructions. Good thing he was friends with Abe Bowman and thought he could work a deal with him that would satisfy his wife without costing him anything. Besides, he needed to pass on the latest word about the possibility of a new war with England.

Rumors had been flying like grackles, flocking through the countryside. The British had been at war with Napoleon for over 10 years and were going to start restricting trade between America and France. You'd think that memories of the colonial revolution would be fresh enough to warn them off, but evidently not.

"Well, old friend, I thank you kindly for your willingness to make this trade. I wouldn't have asked but Millicent insists that Martha isn't suitable as a house slave and you know the house is her domain." He smiled sheepishly at Mr. Bowman. "If we're gonna be having another tussle with the English, I'll need peace in my own house at least. Henry wants to marry her and I'm willing if you are. I know you won't want her son, so I'll keep him now that he can be weaned. When do you want me to bring her over?"

"Give me a couple days to get work assignments redistributed and I'll be ready. Maggie's girl is already working with the girls' team so she can stay with Prissy. Come whenever you're ready; I'll see you later." As Hiram turned to mount his horse and head home, Abraham went in to find his wife and tell her the deal he'd worked out.

On the second day, after lunch, a small wagon pulled up in front of the Bowman house carrying Mr. Barnes and a vaguely familiar young slave woman who looked like she hadn't stopped weeping forever. Her eyes were blood-shot and swollen, her nose dripping, and her face drawn and terrified. Mr. Bowman crossed the yard and opened the gate.

"Here she is, Abe; this is Martha. She's been carrying on like a banshee all morning. I told her I was bringing her here and keeping her son, but she acts like I killed him right in front of her." He stepped down and motioned for the slave to get out too. She scowled darkly but struggled to stand beside the wagon, all the while staring at the ground, refusing to acknowledge either man.

"Come along now, girl. This is your new home and your new massa." At that word, Martha looked up at them, but said nothing. Hiram glanced at Abe and shrugged his shoulders, grabbed Martha by the arm, and pulled her nearer. By that time, Maggie had walked up from her cabin carrying a small bundle, looking as distressed and sullen as Martha. She slid a quick glance at the newcomer.

"I've got my clothes and said good-byes, Massa. I guess I'm ready to go." She peeked again at Martha who was watching her closely.

"Alright. Get on up in Mr. Barnes' wagon. Do what you're told and don't make any trouble." Abe reached out to shake Hiram's hand and the exchange was done. They had their deal and the slaves would just have to get over it. He took Martha down to Binta's cabin and told her to instruct her new housemate in what to do.

* * * *

"I still don't understand why Millicent wanted to give up a perfectly good slave. Martha and Binta are getting along famously and she's been a great help to her. I think Martha has learned the midwife trade very quickly." Mr. Bowman nodded in agreement as he stood with his arm around his wife's waist as they peered down at their youngest daughter sleeping quietly in her trundle bed after having spent the morning careening around the house and then throwing bits of her lunch over the side of her chair, making a mess of the newly cleaned floor. Toddlers were loud, messy, and stinky; maybe it was time to call a halt to having children. "I'm not complaining at all Abraham, you know, but Millicent was a fool to give her up!"

"Well, my dear Margaret, I think the biggest problem is Mrs. Barnes has no patience and it doesn't help that Martha knew only a few dozen words of English when she first came to us. Since Binta's been helping her, she's caught on to what's expected of her."

* * * *

As time passed, the pain of giving up her child lessened somewhat. Martha and Henry were allowed to jump the broom, and he came over on his half day off to report that Ekundayo was growing healthy and strong. Massa Barnes called him Charley, but Titilayo had named him because her sorrow had become joy.

Soon she was expecting another baby and both of them celebrated in spite of their difficult circumstances. By virtue of his consistent good behavior Henry escaped the almost daily whipping sessions at home and was released regularly to visit the Bowman farm once a month. He was particularly proud of his skill at feigning meekness as he had much more freedom of movement than the other men. Getting to spend time with Martha gave him an outlet and a sounding board for his plans for the future. He was well along in working out a sound scheme for escaping forever the Barnes farm and his forced servitude. Secrecy was vital to success. Martha wasn't happy when she considered losing him, but she just couldn't consider leaving her children. She did, however, admire his careful thinking and determination.

Binta and Martha discussed every possible name they might use for the new child. They each had their favorites but would wait to see him or her to make the final decision. Henry had nothing to say about it; this was woman's work.

In late 1810 another son arrived. Martha chose the name Ifedapo because he had been conceived in love, but she also called him Josiah when she had to because that was the name Massa had chosen. She didn't like it, but there was nothing she could do about it.

* * * *

Her next baby was stillborn, a wrenching on-going pain, even though a year later she had another son, whom she named Remi, hoping that eventually he would be her consolation for the baby she and Henry had lost. What kind of a name was Tom, anyway? Of course, there was no arguing with the Massa; everything was as he wanted or else. He tended to yell a lot but seldom got out his whip and she was grateful for small favors.

That Fall and the next Spring a series of violent earthquakes struck western Kentucky frightening people and animals alike for days. It was THE topic of conversation for weeks. Some folks from farther west brought wild tales of massive changes to the flow of the Mississippi River caused by the upheaval. On Sundays the churches were full of folks thanking God for keeping them safe in a time of such panic and dread. The aftershocks slowly subsided and normality reigned once again.

Chapter 6

War Comes to America

The British had begun impressing thousands of American merchant sailors and blockading the Atlantic coast in the Spring of 1812. Then they incited Indian tribes all over the frontier to deadly riot. Congress had finally declared war in June. Now battles were being fought on the Canadian border, all up and down the coast, and out west of the Mississippi. There had been little threat in Kentucky but many men had gone to help under the leadership of Isaac Shelby, previously a soldier in the Revolution and currently Governor of Kentucky. Meanwhile, everyone left at home was on the alert just in case. At least the farming was still moving forward; the army and navy both needed food and provided a ready market.

"Now, Margaret I'm off to visit with Obie over at his place. I want to make sure we have what he wants to trade for his blacksmith's labor. Remember to start keeping an eagle eye on Cook. We can tighten our belts a bit more and sell as much as possible to the government."

He pulled a handful of coins from his pocket, "All this extra cash is right nice to see. I'll send Annie out to the woods with a few of the older slave children to collect as many extra berries, greens, mushrooms, and sorrel as they can gather – make sure you inspect the mushrooms before they're dried; we don't want to take any chances. Once the harvest is over I'll take William and we'll go hunting with Hiram and his sons to stock the larder full for winter."

"Yes, Dear." Margaret had been expecting something of this sort from her husband throughout the current growing season. He had been happily jingling the coins in his pocket since the US Quartermaster had swept through spreading his largesse far and wide. "I absolutely will not, however, starve our children for a few more coppers!"

Mr. Bowman nodded his head in quick agreement, "I wouldn't ever ask you for that, Darling. I know you'll take good care of everyone just as you always do." He smiled benignly at her then turned away and headed down the path to the barn, not noticing the sour look on his wife's face.

"I'm not letting him have all our spare eggs this year, that's for sure!" Margaret mumbled under her breath as she headed out to the summer kitchen to speak to the cook about proper serving sizes to save more supplies for winter; for sure Abraham could afford to shed a few pounds.

* * * *

The War continued to drag on and on. It was exhausting but there seemed to be some progress. The Americans had taken Lake Erie and the western provinces of Canada, but lost the full-on battle for Montreal so they decided to give up trying to capture their neighbors and focus on forcing their enemies to go home <u>again</u>. The British were getting tired too, they were still fighting Napoleon in France as well, and besides it cost a lot of money to keep troops and ships in the field for years at a time. Life on the hill farms continued in spite of the troubles. Day to day, season by season, the work got done, plants grew and were harvested, animals and babies were born and grew healthy.

In August of 1814 Mr. Barnes reported that the new capital of Washington, DC had been captured and burned by the British. Since Pierre Charles L'Enfant, the famous architect and engineer, was back from France, maybe he would create a different design to replace his first version. Then again, they could just re-build using that plan. Earlier this month, the Americans had stopped the invasion of New York, prompting Francis Scott Key to write "The Star Spangled Banner," which was beginning to spread like wildfire. It seemed like the war would never end, but it would, and shortly. The British defeat at Plattsburgh and Jackson's destruction of the Muscogee Nation which finished the Creek alliance at Horseshoe Bend took the heart out of the British army. And now the Canadians were using their victories to start pressing for their own freedom. Of course, no word of these developments had yet spread into the relatively peaceful Kentucky hills.

The Star-Spangled Banner (15 white stars with 8 red and 7 white stripes) was deemed too large for practical use and subsequently abandoned for increasing the number of stars with each new state while retaining the original 7 red and 6 white stripes.

Chapter 7

Martha Gets Her Wish

The heavily Baptist population of Kentucky was just approaching the half million mark, mostly Europeans who had been fleeing persecution in their homelands now joined by nearly eighty thousand Africans, none of whom had come voluntarily. Trees were being cleared as tobacco and hemp became vital cash crops for the families who struggled to make a living on their small hilly farms.

An Overseer Doing His Duty, Benjamin Henry Latrobe. Pen, ink and watercolor sketch, in Martha Washington, Item #26, http://marthawashington.us/items/show/26 (10/13/16).

It was late on that moonlit September night. The pond frogs were competing with the tiny tree peepers for loudest chorus in the neighborhood while crickets added their chirping song to the mix. Two pale reddish cows with their half-grown calves lay under a huge oak tree calmly chewing their cud while four draft horses wandered the field seeking the youngest, most tender grass. It would have been idyllic if only there was even the slightest breeze.

A puncheon log cabin caulked with moss and daubed with mud stood among a small group of its kind on a farm south of the Salt River and west of Clermont. It had a chimney constructed of fire-baked mud and sticks for cooking and heat but little in the way of furnishings—a black kettle sitting on the hearth; a ladle, two plates, two bowls, and two spoons lay on a board shelf; near the fireplace stood a minute table with two narrow ladder-back chairs on either side; and a pallet lay in the corner with a wool blanket draped on a peg above it. The two wool garments on pegs in another wall had two pair of wooden shoes set neatly below them on the bare floor. A lone member of the annual cicada swarm hummed a distinct tune as it wandered the dirt in vain search for a mate. He'd have better luck outside but nobody could take time to set him out by the door in sweltering heat that lingered on from summer. The two women who occupied the single room focused solely on their labor of love. The moon shining through the open doorway provided the only light they had; a fire would have been too much to endure.

Binta and Martha's Cabin on the Bowman Farm.

The dark black slave woman crouched on the floor was more than ready for the imminent arrival of her child. She moaned as softly as her pain would allow. The older woman, who looked enough like her to be her sister, was both her housemate and her midwife. She knelt anxiously beside the laboring young woman, wiping her forehead with a swatch of fresh mint leaves and encouraging her with gentle circular motions to her bulging stomach. In spite of her increasing age and girth, she was still an expert at birthing.

"Remember to keep your teeth tight on the strap, Titi. We don't want to wake our friends who need their rest. And not the Master either as he would surely punish us if his sleep is disturbed. We are both lucky to have come here rather than be sold on that island they call Jamaica." The midwife spoke softly in an unusual language that both understood well. They couldn't do it often, but away from the others they would overcome the cowers and take this chance to speak their own words.

"It is not easy, Binta, but I will be quiet for your sake. I am so glad to have an "aunty" here in this evil land for it is best to follow the old ways in these things. I want only good spirits to attend us." She continued to take deep breaths as she alternately pushed down and relaxed in time with the contractions. In a few moments there was a rush of fluid that was quickly absorbed into the bare dirt.

"Ah, now your baby will come soon, my friend. We must get ready to welcome the new child. I have prepared the knife and the cloth. Let me help you settle over here in this clean place."

The two slowly shifted a few feet closer to the thin, straw-stuffed tick that served as their bed in the corner. A bowl of warm water containing a scrap of faded cloth and a hunk of fine twine, waited nearby a gleaming knife with an edge so sharp it could split hair lengthwise. Binta used a leafy twig to quickly brush loose dirt over the damp spot then lit the little stub of lavender-scented tallow candle she kept handy on the table; she would need more light for her painstaking work.

"Have you chosen a safe place to bury the afterbirth? You have to reach the hiding place and return as soon as you can walk. You must not allow anyone to see you."

"Yes, I can do it." The pains were coming faster and stronger now, so talking was abandoned to the task of pushing as hard as possible. In the age old rhythm, short dark curly hair appeared and disappeared until at last a tiny head broke through. The midwife was ready and reached out swiftly to cradle the head.

"Rest a moment Titi, while I clean the baby's face. One more good hard push should be enough." And so it was. Titilayo sat back, semi-reclined at the very edge of the pallet, resting and watching the midwife at work.

The amniotic fluid and flecks of blood were quickly rinsed away. Then Binta tied off the umbilical cord with two short pieces of twine, sliced it cleanly through the middle with the knife, and placed the little wrinkled body on her mother's chest.

47

"Rub her back while I take care of this." The midwife began to knead a now flaccid abdomen as the baby took her first breaths of life. The two women grinned at each other as the baby squirmed quietly. In short order, the placenta emerged and the bleeding slowed to a thin trickle before stopping completely. The midwife quickly wrapped the bloody pouch and attached cord in a few fern leaves and tucked the stems in to create a compact bundle.

"I am glad to have a baby girl at last. You are so beautiful, my daughter. How I wish that your papa could be here tonight, but we will have to wait until Master Barnes gives him his next half-day. It is good he is just down the road a bit so he does not have to travel far. He is a strong man, but the patrollers are mean as those nasty black mambas at home. They are faster than lightning and their bite is deadly. I miss my home, but I am truly glad you will never meet a mamba in the grass!" Lifting her daughter up into the dim candlelight, Titilayo continued, "Baby girl, I have chosen to name you Ayoke -- you are blessed."

A loud gasp escaped from between the midwife's grim lips as she protested in English. "Nah, nah. Titi, you cannot. You know Massa Bowman wants her name to be Letitia," she smiled slyly and continued, "especially seein' as how she sure can't be Marcus."

Titi smiled too before replying, "Yes, that's true. However, this child must also have a real name. I have decided on Ayoke. Do you have a name in mind? We must keep the traditions of our people, even though we are lost far away from them across the great sea of the Atlantic."

"Now that I have seen her, I think that Dacia would be the right name. Do you not think so too?" Binta asked with another of her sly smiles as she dropped back into their Yoruban dialect.

Gazing softly at her dark-skinned daughter, the new mother smiled broadly at the play on words. "You are right, Binta. She is my little purple flower. Only a tiny bud now, but one day she will blossom into a fine woman."

Titilayo wrapped the newborn in a strip of soft, faded cloth and placed her on the pallet, then grasped Binta's hand in order to stand. She must take up her errand without delay. She was grateful she wouldn't have to go far to secrete the placenta deep under the roots of a huge old tree just on the other side of the pasture. No animal would be able to dig it up and no person would disturb the spirits by finding it either. The midwife then helped her pull on a short wrap-around dress.

"Here, take the afterbirth; I'll hold Letitia so she will not cry. Go quickly and hurry back. We can offer up the water, oil, and salt when you return, and I am sure she will be ready to try your breast after that." The birthing ceremony dated back beyond anyone's memory but had been repeated so many times by the women of so many generations that every step had been committed to memory. It would be followed to the minutest detail according to the ages-old instructions from grandmothers of the most ancient times.

A centuries old family line had reached once again to the next generation. Maybe these weren't the circumstances Titilayo had dreamed of as a young girl, but this was the life that had to be led and they would make the best they could of what they had. There would be good times and bad, joy and sorrow, and most of all, change. America wasn't much older than Titilayo and her people had much to learn.

In early January, Hiram Barnes came firing his pistol and galloping wildly up the road to the Bowman's front gate. As Abraham hurried out the door to discover what the noise was all about, Hiram jumped down and rushed forward to slap him heartily on the back. "The boys will soon be coming home, old friend. Obie Pierce brought word yesterday that the British and Irish signed a peace treaty in December and have gone back to England to get it ratified. The war is over – we beat those rapscallions AGAIN!"

"Lord have mercy. Margaret!" Mr. Bowman cried out for his wife to come quickly. "Margaret, Hiram's brought the best news. The British have given up and gone home. The treaty should be signed and back in Washington by March. The war is finally over!"

Mrs. Bowman hugged her husband and wept copious tears on his shoulder. Then she ran back into the house to tell the others. In two minutes Betsy came racing out the door, dipped a small curtsey to the two men hooting and hollering on the front walk, and continued on toward the slave cabins. Good news traveled fast!

It was time to get back to normal. And they did. Everyone breathed a sigh of relief and went back to their chores. Even the animals seemed happier than usual. The chickens stopped pecking the egg-gatherers every morning and the lambs and calves frolicked in the fields with total abandon. The soldiers and sailors returned in small bunches bringing news of the terrible number of deaths Kentucky had suffered, but a good many weddings that had been postponed the past three years went forward and new couples got engaged. Life was sweet as honey!

* * * *

In the slightly fractured slave version of English, Polly spoke quietly, "Martha, I surely do appreciate you

51

lettin' Callie come stay with you tonight while Binta comes over to our cabin for birthin' my new child." She looked totally relaxed as she led Callie into the tidy room. Of course, this wasn't her first baby, so she felt confident her labor was moving along well.

Binta hastily gathered up her supplies and headed for the door. It was important to get Polly back to peace and quiet where their work would flow along to ultimate success. "Come on, girl! Let's get settled in over to your place, so you can rest. You'll need all your strength tonight!"

"Yes'm. You're startin' to sound just like Martha – in a hurry to go sit around and wait." Binta scowled at her seriously, so Polly smiled at Martha, and sent Callie to sit with Tish on the tick in the corner before following Binta out the door.

"Are you hungry or thirsty, Callie?" Martha asked as she joined the girls.

"No'm."

"How about you, Tish?"

"No, Mama, but I think Sassy is." She held up her rag dolly.

"Oh, that's a really nice baby you've got." Callie held out her doll, "This is Tiny. My Momma gave her to me so we both have a little baby. I told Momma I want a sister, but she says she just ain't sure; it might be a brother. I hope not; I don't want any brother."

"Yeah, brothers are all I've got." Tish looked distraught at the whole notion; she would like to have a sister too but no such luck. Ah well, maybe one day...

"We'll just have to wait and see. Of course, it doesn't matter, you can play with Tish every day while all the mommas work in the tobacco. Tish likes to play with Sassy, feed the calves, chase butterflies, jump in rain puddles, and squish mud with her toes. You both can play gool, ring around the rosie, hide n' seek -- have lots of fun with the other children while you can." Martha, patted each one on the shoulder. They would all start learning their own jobs before too much longer and there wouldn't be much time for playing games.

Chapter 8

Times are Changing

Two years later, Mr. Bowman's acreage under cultivation had slowly expanded as had his small herd of milk cows. Like most Kentucky farmers his herd had consisted solely of hardy Durhams, offspring of the first generation brought from England. Recently, however, Hiram Barnes had been showing off some newly acquired English milk cows called Herefords that he said were much better milk producers. He had offered his prize bull for service to the Bowman cows in exchange for a couple of the mixed-breed calves. It was an exciting prospect that Abraham fully intended to take advantage of at the earliest opportunity. All of his cows had calves of various ages and the oldest could soon be weaned so that their mothers would become receptive to a visit from that bull.

The Bowman team of slaves had also grown, although specialty work was still done by trained slaves hired from larger farms. A small farm like his couldn't afford a slave dedicated solely to blacksmithing or any other area of expertise; everyone had to share the jobs as they had talent.

Durham-Hereford Calf. Cross developed in the early 1800s.

In the neat one-room cabin, Titilayo looked fondly at her daughter, who was busily spooning up her breakfast porridge. She wished heartily she could see Henry again; it was so lonely here without him to hold and commiserate with about life. She had been up in the pre-dawn darkness mixing milk, butter, molasses, and a pinch of salt with ground Indian corn meal and patting it into cakes for cooking.

Now that Tish was almost done eating she could wrap the leftover bread in paper to eat at lunchtime with the pottage left over from supper and kept warm in the pot on the hoe before being ladled into the crocks. Everyone liked the heavy cornbread fried on the hoe which protected the bread from the coals and ash in the fireplace; it didn't take long to make and was tasty and filling, although its mottled black, blue, and red coloring looked somewhat like mold.

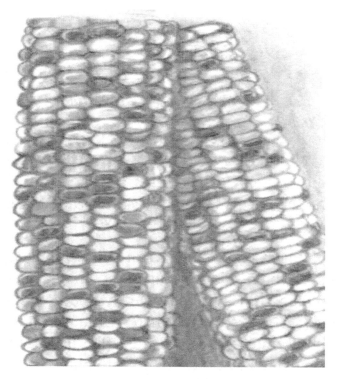

North American Indian Corn or Maize.

Her fried version of a common loaf could be shared because it was larger than journey or hoe cakes, which were fried dry and could be carried while traveling. The cook at the big house made an even larger baked version in her beehive oven, sometimes mixed with a small amount of wheat flour for special occasions, but Titi preferred the plain frying pan style.

"Come along Tish. Don't dawdle over that mush. You're a big girl; it's time you learn your chores. We gotta earn our keep so Massa stay happy and we be happy too." As she looked around her home, Martha added in a whisper, "Just so long as I don't lose another child." One living down the road at the Barnes' farm, one stillborn, two living across the yard in the single larger men's cabin which was full to overflowing; they really needed to build another or at least add on. She missed the boys with a wrenching sorrow; they lived close but they rarely saw each other what with their separate chores. It was her lot in life; there was nothing to be done.

Martha, she thought, how strange it still sounded on her tongue. Titi had slowly grown used to being called by her American name. However, she called her sons by their assigned names only in the presence of the Master or any other white person who might tell him she was using forbidden African names. And she was careful to call her daughter Letitia, but she remembered daily that it wasn't her real name. In her thoughts she'd always be Ayoke Dacia. Maybe she couldn't go home, but she could keep the memories of her tribal traditions alive. At least she got to take Tish with her to the field every day where she could keep an eye on her and be handy to feed her until she had enough teeth and was able to sit at the table with everyone else or until another baby came, which hadn't happened.

Her sons were expected to do a man's work. The men's house, though overcrowded, was for sleeping only; they had a separate cook shack nearby. The two boys cleaned up after breakfast then used it for cooking slops in the great black pots to carry to the pig pens every morning. Afterward they watched over the new piglets to make sure their huge, ponderous mothers didn't crush them. Once they were weaned, the shoats would be moved into a pen of their own to be fattened for slaughter, and the boar would be brought in to start the next generation. Even though her boys were only 7 and 8 years old, they had important jobs.

Today, Martha would help her daughter recognize the dreaded worms that infested the tobacco crop and had to be hunted ruthlessly. She would demonstrate the way to kill them quickly and efficiently. Tish must learn to do expertly as many jobs as possible; a slave's value to the Master was in her abilities, and a talented slave seldom got sold away by her owner – well, except in dire circumstances.

Chapter 9

Work, Work, Work

Martha finished rinsing out their dishes and wiped off the spoons. They would be needed for supper time. The bare minimum was all they had; after all, what else were fingers for? Who needed forks or knives? Although it would be handy, certainly less painful, when there was hot meat for supper. And it sure would be nice to have an extra set of bowls and spoons, but then washing up after every meal helped keep bothersome ants and flies to a minimum too.

Picking up their lunch, she sighed as she reached out to take Tish's hand and headed for the doorway where Binta was just returning with a bucket of clean water. She placed it carefully on the table and scurried out to wave good-bye to her housemates on their way to work.

As they walked along they could hear a ruckus coming from the hen house. All the hens were squawking like a fox had invaded their home. Of course, it was just the two girls assigned to gather eggs this morning. They had already consulted with the cook about the number of eggs she would require for the next 24 hours.

Now they were rummaging in the nests to collect them. Each egg was carefully placed in a straw-lined basket until the right number had been acquired, which was usually relatively large since the eggs were relatively small.

All the eggs were carried to the lean-to outside the chicken yard to be gently wiped clean. Those few that would be stored for later use were coated with rendered tallow, which kept bacteria out and moisture in, then placed in the cask that had been made specifically for this purpose. Eggs coated in this manner and kept tightly covered in a dry place would be safe to use for upwards of a year, if need be, even at room temperature. Since both the Dorkings and the Dominiques quit laying in cold weather it was very handy. This method was much preferred over covering the eggs with salt, wheat bran, or wood ash which not only changed their flavor, but drew moisture out through the shell and spoiled the egg in a matter of a few months.

Letitia didn't really understand all that Momma was saying, but she liked the musical rhythm of her voice when she spoke as they walked along the path in the late Spring sunbeams that had just started peeking over the hill ahead of them. The small family of slaves was headed out to start their morning labors. It was nice to be outside in the fresh air.

Tisha wondered about the brown fuzzy thing with long floppy ears she saw crouched under a flower growing next to the fence; she was sure Momma had told her it was a bunny. It was so funny looking with one eye covered by its oversize ear that she laughed out loud. The startled rabbit jumped straight up and bumped against the flower, knocking drops of dew onto its head, then crouched motionless flat on the ground. Tisha laughed even harder. Immediately, however, she was distracted by the small calf that had come awkwardly galloping to greet them. He had just started eating grass, so Momma grabbed a handful for her to feed to him. She had seen some kind of animal every day as Momma carried her along with the blanket she would sit on while Momma worked, but these days she was walking sturdily on her own two feet over the rough ground. She wished it would rain again so she could squish her toes in the soft, gooey mud. The thought made her giggle impishly.

"What's so funny, missy?" Letitia was pretty sure it wasn't her last comment on the condition of the current tobacco crop.

"Oh nothin', really Momma. It's pretty outside and I'm just happy."

"Humpf. Well, ok then. Let's get goin' again."

It wasn't but a five-minute walk to the tobacco field which lay east of the Bowman house just past the large vegetable garden which contained plants that would supply the family's food for the year. Peas had already formed and several varieties of beans weren't far behind. Carrots and beets had been thinned a couple of times and looked to be a bumper crop coming on. This early, corn was up about knee-high but had not even the beginnings of the one or two ears each stalk would produce. Early potatoes and squash varieties were quickly spreading out in the warm sunshine which had finally crept over them. Before long, the later crops, like pumpkins and onions would be added to the mix. Enough food had to be grown to keep starvation at bay come winter.

The older children were already on duty here too, moving slowly among the different crops checking diligently for and killing the bugs and caterpillars that could ruin a crop in a matter of hours. Cutworms, earworms, hornworms, cabbage loopers, root maggots, vine borers, and a host of voracious beetles were their daily enemy throughout the growing season. The work wasn't difficult and they all enjoyed this time to visit with the children from other cabins.

Cheerful conversations could be heard from every section of the garden, sometimes interrupted by barely muffled laughter over some silly joke or quip about one workmate or another. At 9 and 10 years of age, neither the group of girls nor the separate boys' group had much interest in the other, except as the subject of disparaging comments. Martha sighed. Oh, to be so young and carefree again…

Martha quit thinking about vegetables as another woman came into view and Tish shouted, "Mornin' Tabitha."

Martha also called, "Mornin'. We'll be workin' together today since Binta's takin' her turn at doin' the washin'." She smiled as her friend grinned slightly and nodded her head. Tabitha had cocoa-colored skin and a broader, rounder face. She didn't know where she had come from in Africa, and none of them recognized her accent or any of the words she spoke. Not that it mattered, of course, they were all learning English as best they could; Massa didn't allow any of their foreign talk. Although he had allowed Binta her name, since her previous owner had let her use it and it was easier to continue than trying to teach her a new one at her age.

"I'm glad to be out here. I don't want to be in that shed with all that steamin' water on such a nice day. We each have to help, but I say she can have that job for as long as she's able. Jonah says Massa Barnes has got a slave who doesn't do anythin' but wash the clothes and beddin' and such, and hang them out to dry, then iron up the shirts and linens for that whole big family all day long. He says she hardly has time to sit and enjoy a morsel now and then. It's no wonder she's so skinny. That's gotta be miserable."

Martha nodded in agreement. "Miss Tish here is gonna be a farmer this mornin'. She'll be five right soon and that's old enough to start learnin'." She slowed and looked down at Letitia. "I know Henry would be proud of his little girl. I just wish he hadn't been so set on runnin'. I know it wasn't but a few months back but it seems like he's been gone forever. He was smart to go after the ground had dried out so his footprints wouldn't show where he was headin'. I suppose he's safe up North somewhere or we'd have never heard the end of it from Massa Barnes.

"Hooee, he was jumpin' up and down mad as an old wet hen when he came by to tell Massa Bowman what went on in the early mornin' hours that day. He couldn't see anythin' in the dark before dawn. By the time he got the patrollers out with their bloodhounds, there was nothin' but a scent trail all the way to the Ohio River. He was so red in the face I thought he was gonna fall down in a fit right there on the doorstep. I could hardly keep from laughin' at him."

"You best hush now, Martha. You don't want Massa Bowman to hear you talkin' about such things. He'd take a strap to you and you know it."

"Oh, I know it for sure. I been strapped often enough; I don't want to see that leather again any time soon. Let me show Tish how to find and kill those tobacco worms. Then I'll help you get the weeds hoed out from between the rows. Won't be long and we'll be pickin' off the flowers. Get that done and it's nearly time to start cuttin' the leaves for dryin'. Tobacco grows so fast we can't hardly keep up."

"Alright. I'll get started over here so we can be near to keep eyes on her. Don't want her gettin' into anythin' dangerous." Not that there were a lot of dangerous critters around. Most of the worst predators had been hunted out or fled the hills for the wilderness farther west. Still there was an occasional black bear or bobcat and plenty of fox and snakes--copperheads and kings, even rattlers in the woodlands. One couldn't be too vigilant when children were involved.

Tabitha and Martha with Machetes Ready for Work.

Martha guided Tish to a row of smallish tobacco plants. "Squat down and look at this leaf here." She held it up in the air so they could see the bottom side. "There isn't a worm on this one. So look at this one here," she said as she lifted up one leaf after another. Then she pointed to the next plant. "Be gentle. Hold the leaf up so you can see it good."

As Tish lifted up the first leaf, Martha noted, "Aha, see that big green wiggly thing with black and white stripes and little red horn? That's a worm and he's bad. Grab him like this and pinch his tummy hard." She demonstrated what needed to happen, and Tish giggled as the worm gushed out his shiny yellow innards.

"Now, scoot on down here to the next plant and look beneath it. Is there a worm?" She clapped her hands in approval as Tish looked, grabbed, and pinched just as Momma had done. "Good girl. You're just a bitty scrap, but you're smart and strong. You keep on doin' that while I go help Tabitha with hoein'. I'll be close by and will come get you when it's time to rest and have a drink of water."

"Alright Momma." Tish was busy scooting along the row to the next plant. Mushing worms was almost as much fun as squishing mud. She wished that Callie could have come with them, but she was back at her cabin helping her Momma take care of their newest baby.

Martha and Tabitha were a good team; their hoes flew over the ground in well-timed strikes at the new grown weeds. Every 15 minutes, Martha went over a row to check on Tish. Sometimes, she needed help sticking to her task, but other times she focused on doing her job. Martha was proud of her daughter and looked forward to one day having another husband who could give her more children. She wanted a large extended family like her mother had enjoyed before the Fula had swept away her life. Ah well, there was no going home even if she could figure out which way to start walking. She remembered just how far it was from here to the North Carolina coast and then nothing could be done in the face of the great sea. Runners seldom got far and the thought of being whipped stirred up a storm of cowers. It was more than enough incentive to stay in this place where her children were close by.

After two hours, Tabitha leaned over and whispered, "Let's take a break and go give Tish some more water; I've got news for you." They scurried over to the water bucket which sat in the deep shade of the ancient oak at the edge of the field and each had a dipper full before Martha carried it over to where Letitia was trying to capture a butterfly; apparently one of the early caterpillars had escaped the daily hunt and survived to transform itself into the brown insect with small, pale orange spots that was flittering just out of reach of Tish's grasping fingers.

"Come sit and let Momma help you to a cool drink." She knelt down to offer the water, which Tish slurped at greedily. "So, what's the news?" She queried as she glanced up.

After a quick look around, Tabitha said in a hushed voice, "You know the Simpson farm on the other side of the hill behind Massa Bowman's house? Well, it seems a family has moved in and they brought eight or 10 men with them to work the new hemp field they've got planned. I hear they're all young, strong, and good lookin'." Tabitha wiggled her eyebrows up and down as she continued, "Maybe I can get me a husband now like you had before Henry run off. What do you think of that?"

"Hooee, sounds good to me, although I sort of doubt they're ALL so temptin'. You're a good cook and sure enough a catch for any man. You think he'll come live with us?"

"Martha, I just heard the rumor; I don't know anythin' for sure. I know it was hard on you havin' to live apart from Henry like you did, but I'll be happy to have a husband any way I can get him. At least the Simpson place is a lot closer."

"Yeah, I suppose any which way is better than none at all. Come on, let's get the rest of this section done; we're gettin' behind the other team! We can eat lunch later."

Early that evening Martha filled Binta in on the gossip she'd heard from Tabitha then speculated on the news as they slowly ate their supper of fried squirrel and dandelion greens. It was fortunate that Kentucky squirrels were so large compared to those in other places. And dandelions grew wild and free for the picking along with onion grass, prickly lettuce, and watercress. A couple of fresh-skinned squirrels and a mess of greens meant they all ate well.

"Let's go find out if Tabitha and Sally have heard anythin' else about the new neighbors."

"Alright Martha. But if Massa catches us out sneakin' around he's gonna be havin' a fit."

"Don't be silly Binta. It isn't even dark yet. Why would he worry about what we're doin' when he can see us plain as daylight and we're only goin' next door?" Martha glanced over at her sleeping daughter.

"Lookee there. Tish's sound asleep already. Guess she's gonna miss out on her regular visit with Callie. She sure enough had a long first day workin' and got plumb tuckered out. Don't waste any time fussin'; let's get goin' and back before Massa knows what we're doin'!"

Sally and Tabitha were still scrubbing out their dishes when Binta and Martha hurried through the doorway of a little cabin that could have been the twin to theirs. The furniture was slightly different, they had two little benches instead of chairs, but everything else looked exactly the same. As the weather got warmer they had begun picking the chinking out of the walls; it allowed for some movement of air for cooling and could be easily replaced with more mud and moss in the Fall to help hold in heat through the Winter.

"Have you heard anythin' more about the new family over the hill?" Martha blurted out her question as she plopped down on one of the benches.

"Well, good evenin' to you too Miss Martha. Sure is nice to see you again. Why don't you sit on down and join us in a cup of tea? Would you like a bite of honey on some bread and butter?" The two roommates watched their visitor out of the corners of their eyes as they tried unsuccessfully to keep from laughing at her consternation.

"Oh, you women think you're so funny, don't you? Miss Martha indeed. "Humpf! Just for that, I do believe I will have a bit of tea and sweetness. And while I'm waitin' for you to serve it up, I want an answer to my question. Come on over and have a seat here Binta." Martha patted the other bench. "They're gonna feed you a treat too." It was good to relax and laugh with friends after a long day in the field. In a couple of hours it would be dark and they would need to get to bed so they could be ready for more of the same tomorrow, and the next day, and the next.

Unfortunately, neither of their friends knew any more than they did about the newcomers. They waited patiently for the water to boil and then gathered around the little table, taking turns sipping from the cups and passing the tiny plate of bread and honey to one another. This possibility for acquiring husbands was an exciting topic of conversation, much better than the usual after supper fare. When that subject was exhausted they went on to every tidbit of gossip they'd been able to scrounge recently.

Sally mentioned casually, "Betsy told me Missus Pierce told Mrs. Bowman she heard from Missus Campbell that according to her husband he thought our neighbor Mr. Prenzlau had been a horse thief up in Virginia. A half dozen really fine horses were stolen in the month before they moved down to the farm."

That was an astonishing revelation to say the least. There had been no word of such things happening since they arrived in Kentucky so maybe it wasn't true after all. Fine horse flesh had been far more common in Virginia than in Kentucky until they began racing in Lexington and Louisville in the 1780s. Then both Thoroughbreds and Arabians began to be bred in 1800.

In fact, the Lexington area was exploding with racing horse farms and more were springing up west toward Frankfort and south toward Danville to feed the racing frenzy being spurred on by the 10-year-old Jockey Club and investors in various private and public tracks.

Martha looked vaguely skeptical. "Well, I don't know all that much about the man, so I guess I'll wait and see. Maybe he's a thief and maybe he isn't. Maybe he's given up his bad ways." Or maybe he'd go back to his old ways as the horse population grew around here. Who knew?

"Well," Binta piped up in a smug tone. "I heard from Betsy just this mornin' that Massa's gonna be sendin' Polly back out to the tobacco field in another week. That's good news for all of us. She'll be takin' both Callie and her baby girl with her, so she can nurse whenever she needs to. What'd she name that baby anyway? Sarah somethn'? No, I remember, Sarella."

"I kinda like that name; it's almost the same as mine. You think Massa is gonna let her keep it?" Sally looked doubtful as she contributed to the conversation. There were shrugs all around in answer to her question.

"It'll be nice to have everyone together again, even though it isn't easy havin' such a tiny child in the field. Course, we've all done it more than once so I guess they'll make do." Martha sat back with a satisfied smile. It was nice to just sit still for a bit. "I like the idea of switchin' out work partners too. I mean, I love all of you like sisters, but it'll be nice for Tish to have a friend her own age to work with. She's been kinda lonesome since Callie's been stayin' home with Polly. Of course, she stops by to chat and play almost every night before supper. Those girls are closer than twins!"

The others all knew exactly what she meant. Nobody liked working alone. Every job went faster and was less boring when you had a companion to share with. In another couple of years the little children would be forming their own teams to work in the vegetable garden and another couple after that and they'd have their own jobs to fill in the tobacco fields if they weren't drafted for the chicken shed. It was to their advantage but hard to think about them growing into independence.

Finally, Martha and Binta rose, hugged their friends, said their good-byes, and hurried off to their cabin to check on Letitia, who was still sleeping soundly and now snoring lightly. They took turns going out to take care of their nightly constitutional and were ready to huddle on the tick, glad to have three bodies to help keep themselves warm until Summer arrived.

Chapter 10

All the Comforts of Home

"Martha, Tabitha. Get on out here you two."

At the sound of Mr. Bowman's call, the two women hurried out of their cabins to stand before their owner on the little dirt path between the two. The hovering cowers caused trembling in their legs. Apprehension was strong in their hearts and on their faces — you just never knew what might happen when the Master was calling you first thing in the morning and had a short, thin stranger, dressed in every day working clothes, standing beside him staring at you like you were a breakfast hoe cake. This didn't look good.

"This here is Mister Prenzlau," Mr. Bowman hesitated slightly at pronouncing the foreign name. "He bought the Simpson place over yonder. We made a deal for a couple of his field hands to come on over here after they've done their chores to spend evenings with you. Whichever of you catches first will go over to his place and help out until your child is weaned. So, you see to it that you treat them good and get yourselves with child right quick." He looked vaguely embarrassed at saying such things and quickly added, "Now, get on down to the field and get to work."

After moving away only a couple of steps Mr. Bowman wheeled around toward the women and raising his voice, reminded them, "Tell those boys of yours to keep on collecting all the fireplace ash and dumping it in the little shed over at the vegetable garden. We're going to need every bit we can get together to keep that garden producing at high yield. As we have more folks to feed we need to expand our capacity." At that, he turned to Mr. Prenzlau with a nod, "Gotta keep on top of every little thing every day or we'd be in a mess for sure."

The two men began again to walk away without another glance at the stunned women, but they continued their conversation. "I think this plan'll work out well for us both Mr. Prinslow." Mr. Bowman had already lost track of how to say his unusual-sounding name. Lots of folks had strange names in this new country. Eventually they were bound to all settle on something that was more easily pronounced, at least he sure hoped so.

The women stared at their retreating backs. "Well, that's not what I was lookin' for. Guess we aren't gonna get husbands after all. What do you think, Martha?"

"I think we've got no choice in the matter. I think we're gonna have company for supper tonight and every night whether we like it or not. You think he'd let me take Tish with me if I have to go live over the hill? I sure don't want to leave her, but I know you and Binta'll take good care of her."

"Oh Martha. Let's not look for trouble that might never raise up its ugly head. We'd best get on down to the field before Massa Bowman sees us standin' around like we've got nothin' to do." As she grabbed up the hoe from next to her doorway, Tabitha muttered one of Martha's favorite sayings, "I can't see this turnin' out good for anybody but the Massa, that's for sure.

"I wonder what kind of name that man's got, it's not hardly English!" And it wasn't, of course. David's grandfather had come from eastern Europe, he thought from Germany or maybe Poland; the land and its citizens had been rearranged after each of the many wars that had been fought in Europe. Family ties were fading more quickly than accents over time and distance.

Two young black-eyed, pecan-colored men arrived at the Bowman farm in the waning light of dusk. Muscles bulged in arms and legs; one could tell they were accustomed to hard physical labor. They went to the main house and waited nervously near the front porch until Mr. Bowman came out to escort them to the slave quarters where he pointed to the proper shacks.

Tabitha and Martha also waited nervously in the doorways. They each greeted one another with a nod and a shy smile. Then they exchanged names as the women ushered the men in to where supper was waiting on the tables. They managed to make small talk until they gradually grew more comfortable with each other. They would work in the fields by day and spend nights in cozy comfort with their new friends. None of them got to choose, but it was a sort of joy to once again be in the presence of someone who didn't yell at them or beat on them and whose eyes gleamed with interest, kindness, and delight. This wouldn't be onerous duty after all.

Letitia frequently went over to Polly's after dinner to spend the evening playing with Callie. Callie's skin was such a strange color, the palest brown she'd ever seen, almost like caramel taffy candy. Well, except for her older brother who lived on Massa Barnes' farm and even his was a bit darker than hers. She didn't really mind, but it was strange. The girls had their faceless rag dolls that they talked with constantly. These were their babies; they had proper names and were carried everywhere and rocked before being put to bed for the night.

In the warm weather they really loved to sit on the creek bank to dangle their feet in the cool water. Sometimes the little fish came and nibbled on their toes, which tickled something fierce and sent them into gales of squealing laughter. Of course, mud squishing was high on their agenda too. Polly always made sure the girls washed away the mud and got to bed when darkness fell so they wouldn't be too tired the next morning.

And Jeremy was so sweet; he went with Martha to Polly's and gently carried Letitia home to their bed before he and Jack hustled back over the hill. On moonless nights they carried a torch to light their way and as a signal to Mr. Prinslow that they had returned as expected and would be ready for work the next day.

* * * *

"Tabitha, are you sure? It's been hardly more than a month since Jack's been comin' over nights and you haven't even got any mornin' heaves yet. I'm gonna miss you somethin' fierce. I just can't believe Massa Bowman's gonna send you over the hill. What're you gonna do over there? Are you gonna cook for all Massa David's field hands? At least you won't be totin' your baby any farther than the vegetable garden if you're the cook. I suppose you'll be scrubbin' the clothes too and helpin' Missus Rebecca at her house seein' as how she does have the heaves already. Don't scowl so. She told the Missus and the Missus told the Massa; I heard her. Makes me tired just thinkin' about all the work you're gonna have to do, and Jeremy hasn't even given me a baby yet."

"Heavens, Martha. You don't give me a breath to get a word in any which way! Yep, I'm pretty near sure. I should have had my monthlies last week. Besides, I've never had the heaves when I've had a baby comin'. And how do I know what I'm gonna be doin'? I'll just have to hie myself over there and find out. I'm probably gonna work the hemp like everybody else, at least while I can still get around. I'm glad you're gonna stay here with Tish; she needs her momma close. And I wouldn't worry any about Jeremy; he's got plenty of energy for givin' you a baby any ole night." At this, both women covered their mouths and giggled until they fell to the ground in a heap. There weren't any secrets between them, living in such close quarters and all. It was so good to have best friends to work and eat and sleep and laugh with. Too bad there wasn't any offer of the choice of a husband, not that they really expected one. You just did what the Massa said whether you liked it or not. It had to be done. At least it wasn't an unpleasant chore like some that had to be endured in the past.

That night she thought once again of the children she rarely saw any more. Why would the Massa keep her family separated from one another? It wasn't right; children needed their mother. Very few families lived all together in the same cabin on the same farm.

Almost every slave she knew lived in the same circumstances she did. "Guess the Massas are all alike, but it still makes no sense." It was her last thought before sleep overwhelmed her.

A few weeks later when Jeremy came for his nightly visit he had unhappy news. "Massa says he's thinkin' maybe he's wastin' time hopin' for gettin' another slave out of us. We're takin' too long havin' a baby. He says he told Massa Bowman I gotta stay home and work more hours in the hemp."

"Oh, Jeremy, I can't bear the idea that we might never see each other again." He kissed her tear-streaked cheeks and whispered what reassurance he thought might ease her sorrow. They clung to one another, saddened by the thought of losing their time with each other and their chance for friendship.

Later Jeremy had a mysterious story to tell. "Last night after I got back to the farm I was talkin' with Jack. I gotta tell you he's so happy to have Tabitha livin' over near to us where they can see each other every day and soon she'll have his new baby. Anyways, we heard a bunch of horses ploddin' into the barnyard so we sneaked a peek out the doorway to see who was comin' in the middle of the night. There was three strangers ridin' horseback, each leadin' two other horses.

Hemp Harvest on the Prinzlau Farm.

The Massa came tiptoein' out of his house and was whisperin' with 'em but we heard most everythin'. They'd been travelin' every night for more than a week makin' their way across Kentucky from Lexington headin' for Missouri. Massa gave them each a drink and a couple of sandwiches so he must have been waitin' for 'em. While they were eatin' he told 'em how to find an ole cabin in the woods a few miles farther west where they could stay over before they ride out again tomorrow night. He said they were doin' good keepin' quiet and out of sight. Those were mighty showy horses they were leadin' along. Why do you suppose he thinks they want to be hidin' out?"

"Probably best if you don't be askin' such things, Jeremy. I surely don't want you gettin' into trouble even if you don't get to visit me anymore. Best you get yourself on back over the hill. If I don't see you tomorrow for supper I'll know your Massa has forbid it. I'll be awful sad because it's been a comfort to have you for a friend these months. Maybe we'll see each other again if we come for a birthin'." She took his hand as they got up from the tick and walked slowly along the path toward Polly's cabin.

"You go on now, while I fetch Letitia." She hugged him tightly once again and waved her fingers until he disappeared into the darkness before she made her way to Polly's and carried her daughter back to their cabin to sleep. Why? Why couldn't they have been married? A baby would have come along, she was sure of it. As she mourned for their lost opportunity, sleep overtook her too and she dreamed of having her family together again.

* * * *

"Massa, Massa. Prissy fainted down at the tobacco field. She's lookin' mighty poorly. We poured cool water on her face, but she isn't comin' around." Polly was in a totally panic-stricken state when she finally reached Mr. Bowman who had stood up from his porch rocking chair where he'd been fanning himself in the summer heat.

Bowmans' Limestone Farmhouse.

"Come along here, girl. I'm guessing she's got a mite of heat stroke and I've got something that will help her." He led the way down to the creek and pulled at a twine string attached to a jug sitting on the creekbed. "This ginger switchel will bring her back; just give her a few sips and see if she comes around. If not, try a few more, but get Bill and Moses to move her over under the big oak tree at the edge of the field. When she starts reviving, give her a dipper of water out of the bucket. A bit of rest and she'll be good as new. Get on back quick as you can." Mr. Bowman shooed her toward the tobacco field and headed back to his house.

When he got most of the way there he shouted, "Betsy. Get on down here." When she appeared on the porch and hurried toward him, he began giving her instructions. "I need you to take a message to Mrs. Bowman. Tell her I'm gonna need her to make up another jug of ginger punch. Get some fresh water in the big jug and find two empty small ones, the Barbados molasses, the apple cider vinegar, and the box of powdered ginger out of the pantry. Oh, and grab the recipe box from the cupboard and take everything to the kitchen table. Then find my wife.

"Once she gets it all mixed together good, she can divide it between the two small jugs. Put one jug in the root cellar and tie up the other down at the creek in case any of the field hands need it again. And tell the rest of the workers to keep an eye on any of the slaves that are lighter-skinned like Prissy. I know you all don't feel it too often, but this heat is enough to knock over a horse." After she disappeared he mumbled to himself, "She'd better not die. I surely don't want to lay out good money to buy another slave."

Mr. Bowman slowly made his way back to the porch. Even in the heavy shade provided his wife's thick wisteria vines, it was still stiflingly warm. He decided he better take his glass inside for some cool water; he'd have to get it himself since Betsy would be busy helping Margaret in the kitchen and then delivering the newly made elixir.

He hated going into the house during afternoons like today's. Once the nightly cold had seeped out of the stones throughout the morning, the temperature rose quickly. Even with every window open the lack of a steady breeze didn't help keep the house livable. Thank heavens the cook had already moved out to the shack for the summer or the whole household would be needing daily doses of the restorative switchel!

Chapter 11

Year In, Year Out

Summer blended into Fall and Fall into Winter. Letitia and Callie took advantage of the shorter, slower work days to get sewing instructions and assistance from their mothers. Each had planned a project for the other for Christmas Eve.

"Momma, I think Callie will really like the dress we're makin' for Tiny. She doesn't have any clothes for her just like Sassy doesn't have any. After Christmas do you think we can make a dress for Sassy too?"

"Well, Tisha, we'll just have to wait and see." Martha knew that Polly was already helping Callie construct a simple garment to give to Tish for her doll. She didn't want to make any unnecessary promises.

The girls were each absolutely delighted to receive a tiny colorful apron for her special doll along with a molasses cookie from the cook up at the big house. Christmas came and went with lots of cold wind but without the normal snowstorms.

Mr. and Mrs. Bowman had been especially generous on Christmas morning, granting everyone the entire day off and handing out coins to all the slaves. The large baked ham and yams with molasses were enough for everyone to share. For once, friends, both young and old, spent the day visiting, eating, and napping just like all the Bowmans were doing.

The day after the New Year was ushered in with fireworks, gunshots, and much hoorahing, Tish sidled up to her Mother and held out her clenched fist. As she tipped her hand over Martha's outstretched palm, she said shyly, "Momma I want you to keep my money safe for me. Someday I will have collected enough to buy my freedom and I know I need to start now. I would very much like to move over the Ohio River where we all can live free." Momma wanted freedom but couldn't have it, so Tish would get it for her.

Martha was totally stunned to hear this declaration from such a young girl. Still, Tisha had always been one to think for herself, so it shouldn't really surprise her. "Well, that's a wonderful plan, child. Of course, I'll find a really good hidin' place. We'll just see what we can do to make your plans come true as time goes by."

* * * *

Mr. and Mrs. Bowman had been to the village of Clermont to do some much needed shopping. After a housebound winter, Mrs. Bowman enjoyed the good weather and chance to travel monthly to natter with neighbors and show off her well-made finery even if it was just a day dress in cotton gingham. Mr. Bowman looked upon his visit to the distillery as the essential stop. Jim Beam® was fast becoming a household name in the region and he was bound to run into a friend or two. Catching up on the news was important and all the men kept a healthy supply of whiskey in the pantry in case a friend should stop in later. As their wagon bumped its way south nearing home, they saw another heavier farm wagon making its way slowly toward them.

Leonard Cagle's Farm Wagon.

"Well, Mother, look who's coming. It's someone we know." As they drew closer, he called out.

"Hello, Mr. Cagle. I haven't seen you in weeks. Where have you been? You've not been sick have you?" The two drivers brought their mules to a staggered halt so they could easily speak to each other across the wagon sides.

"Nein, nein; I am well. You know my eldest sons, Lindsey and Henry?" He indicated the two teens sitting beside him on the wagon seat. At a nod from Mr. Bowman, he went on. "We are returning from Missouri. We have been to Carthage to find a place to build a dairy. I fear there will be trouble with the abolitionists up North, so I will take my ehefrau and my family farther west in hope that we will find peace. My neighbor, René LaForce, is taking his family there also." Not able to see the future, Mr. Cagle had no idea that René's granddaughter Rhoda would marry his youngest, as yet unborn, son Willis some years yet to come.

"Now, Leonard, don't go looking for trouble. Yes, those abolitionists are downright disgusting idiots, but they need our cotton and tobacco crops which means we need our slaves, so I don't think they'll actually try to mess in our business any more than they already have. Besides, what've we got to fear from them darned Yankees? We're just as tough and certainly feistier. We can lick 'em good if it comes down to a shooting war."

"Yah, yah. I know all the arguments. My Grossvater was forced to flee from Germany almost 100 years ago. Drury Smith, Elizabeth's father, fought in the Revolutionary War, as did René when he was just a young sprossling. We all support freedom.

"My boys and I are all I need to keep our dairy thriving. David is very young now but he will grow big and strong like his four older brothers. I have no use for slaves. Besides, there are too many people here in Kentucky. I want to find land enough that all my boys can bring their wives and children to live near me and Elizabeth in our old age. We will need much space for our growing klungel."

The two families abruptly waved farewell, flicked impatient reins at the mules, and continued on their way toward their respective homes.

"I just don't understand his attitude." Abraham grumbled to his wife after they were out of earshot of the other wagon. "Honestly Margaret, if we don't fight for our rights, who's going to? Those Northerners think we're a bunch of ignorant hicks, but we're not. We're good hard-working Christians. We know the

Bible, and slaves just aren't our equals. It's our bounden duty to rule over those folks as humanely as possible, but we still have to make sure they do a full day's work every day and earn their keep. Besides, every state has a sovereign right to make and enforce its own laws. The federal government needs to mind its own business, not ours."

Mrs. Bowman nodded sympathetically and patted her husband's arm. These discussions had been going on for many years and she didn't expect to hear the end of them anytime soon. She had far more important things to ruminate on, the social gossip of central Kentucky occupied her time and energies. Which young couples were courting, which family was soon to host a wedding, who was planning a barn dance, who was showing signs of increasing the local population — these were fascinating topics, unlike boring crops, politics, and weather the husbands all seemed to cherish.

In the meantime, Mr. Cagle was shaking his head sadly and talking gently to his boys. "Sohne, I want you to understand why I cannot agree with our friends and neighbors here in Kentucky and all over the South. All men are subject to the rule and instruction of their government and employers, of course, but to force anyone to work under threat of harm is wrong. My Opa farmed in Obermehlingen in Germany, but he brought his family to Pennsylvania to escape persecution. I cannot justify nor condone persecution of others." He shook his head again.

"Now, we must hurry home to help your Mama and the girls pack up so we get settled in Missouri before the new baby arrives. I know Momma would like to have another girl, but I'm hoping for another son to help us with the milk cows." The two boys nodded their heads judiciously and murmured their agreement with that sentiment. Another pair of hands to help manage their growing herd would certainly be welcome even if it would be several years before a new brother would actually be capable of aiding with the milking mornings and evenings.

* * * *

Tabitha returned to the Bowman farm distraught at having to leave both Jack and her son behind, but she was partly cheered by the idea that at least the two of them would be together. She took the first opportunity to visit Martha and Binta with news that she'd picked up months ago from Jack. This story had to be conveyed in secret and kept from anyone else in case it escaped into some massa's ears. So they sent Letitia up to play with Callie while the three women sat in the cabin.

"I been just waitin' for this chance to tell you all what happened last year right around the time my Junior came squallin' into your hands, Martha – sorry there wasn't enough time while you were there. A big bunch of strangers come ridin' hard from Louisville way led by this loud ole sheriff. They were all riled up talkin' with Massa Prinslow for a long time, then they dragged out all the men slaves and asked them lots of questions too. We were all scared half to death! Finally, they got so disgusted they told 'em they were givin' up the hunt and goin' back to Lexington. Then they stampeded off eastwards."

The women stared at each other, eyes wide and breathing hard. "Oh Tabitha, what happened?" Martha's voice quaked as she asked her question tentatively, even though she was pretty sure she knew what the invasion had been about.

"Well, Jack came to have supper and he told me the whole story. Seems there were some fancy racin' horses stolen from a farm near to Lexington. They were supposed to be hidden somewhere in Louisville. So the sheriff got together his two deputies and this big ole posse and went ridin' after those thieves. They found nary a trace in Louisville so they kept huntin' south 'til they got to Massa Prinslow's place.

None of our people saw nor heard anythin' they wanted to share so they just said they don't know anythin' and Massa Prinslow said that too. Those posse men were mad enough to start shootin' but the sheriff decided it wouldn't do any good so they headed off to home. Jack says he and Jeremy did see those thievin' fellows talkin' with the Massa and he seemed to know them. They ate and watered those horses and the Massa sent them off west toward Missouri. But they knew if those men didn't whip 'em bad, the Massa would and probably kill 'em so they kept it all secret. What do you all think about that? It seems Massa Prinslow IS a horse thief like we suspected!"

"Well, it does appear so." But that was all Martha was willing to chance. She wondered silently if Massa Prinslow had told Massa Bowman about the sheriff's visit. There'd been no hint of rumors so maybe he was keeping it quiet. No sense, after all, to get the neighbors speculating when it wasn't needful. "Guess we'd best get to sleep." Better for all that this story be forgotten as soon as possible!

Chapter 12

Moving Right Along

Binta and Martha gathered up their birthing supplies and tools after the supper dishes were done. At the Prinslow's house, a new baby would be arriving in the night and Mr. Prinslow had insisted that they be available early to ensure a safe labor and birth. This would be Letitia's third delivery as their assistant. She hated to give up her evening which was usually spent hostessing a visit from Callie. However, she really looked forward to this learning opportunity. Tish was attentive and industrious, a great help with the midwifing work, making sure the proper supplies were in place and ready to be used at the proper time, while Momma and Binta focused their energies on the mother and child. She had earned a small mound of coins to add to her growing collection and was eager to find ways to bring in more.

"Come along now." As usual, Martha was impatient to get moving. "That baby won't wait for us to lollygag our way over the hill. We certainly don't need Missus Prinslow upset by any unpleasantness from that husband of hers. You know he'd complain to the Massa in a heartbeat."

"Yes, M'am. I'm comin' as fast as these ole legs can hustle." Binta grinned widely as she needled Martha.

"Don't you m'am me," Martha retorted. "Let's just get along out the door. You too, Tish."

"Yes, Momma. I've got the new lavender candle safe in my apron pocket. I'm ready to head out."

"It's about time. You're as slow as one of those bitty box turtles or maybe even a snail. That baby's Momma is gonna need help as soon as we get there, this bein' her fourth child. I told Massa Bowman that we'd be back by mornin'. I don't suppose it's gonna take long."

Of course, it would take however long it took. One never knew what delays might appear during a birth. Sometimes labor was slow going. Sometimes the baby had refused to turn head down. Sometimes the mother labored so long she ran out of energy and the baby had to be helped out. Every birth was different; a midwife had to be prepared for anything, and Tish was going to be one of the best in Kentucky, she was sure.

As they hurried along the trail to the Prinslow's farm, Martha thought back over the many births she had attended. The arrival of a new child was such a joyful occasion. Only in the instance of a stillbirth was the job a tragedy; she really hated losing a child and/or the mother! That thought caused her to remember her own dead baby. You never got over a loss like that no matter how many children you eventually had. She shook her head at herself. Best not to be thinking bad thoughts at a time like this. No point in getting distracted or inviting bad luck…

* * * *

Not even a month went by before Mr. Prinslow visited the Bowman farm with surprising news. He and his wife were packing up their household and moving on west. "I surely do hate to give up my fine farm, but those strangers just got me too dang riled up. I'll be darned if I'll live here and have my home invaded by crowds of loud-mouthed ruffians waving guns in my face. Don't know where they got the notion that I might know anything at all about somebody else's missing horses. I got enough of my own animals to deal with. At any rate, there's plenty of good farming land in Missouri and we're gonna take advantage. You've been a good neighbor, Abe. You ought to think about headin' out too."

"Well, I thank you for the compliment, David, but we're a mite old for starting over in a new place. I think we'll just stay here and let you young folks go off to see the elephant on your own. You leavin' soon?"

"Yep, we're ready to head out now. I just wanted to come by and let you know we're goin' and wish you and your family the best. We'll be lookin' for land near the River up toward Weston. If you change your mind, look us up."

"I doubt that'll happen, but I'll surely keep it in mind. You all take care now." Mr. Bowman tossed off a short wave of his hand as he turned to go inside to advise his family of this unexpected news.

"Oh, we will." Mr. Prinslow waved his hat as he brought his horse around toward the hill trail.

The Bowman slaves, who had been standing around their cabins talking quietly while they listened to the two men, then gathered together to discuss the Prinslows' sudden decision to leave Kentucky. Binta, Martha, and Tabitha kept their lips tightly sealed around what they knew, but they wondered how in the world Missus Prinslow was going to travel with that brand new baby. It wasn't something a person did unless there was danger threatening. Maybe they were afraid someone else would come looking for "lost" horses, someone who might shoot first and ask questions later....

Mrs. Prinslow had slipped a few small coins into Letitia's hand once her new son was safely ensconced in his cradle which stood next to the bed where she lay exhausted but resting comfortably. She had also passed a larger one to Binta and another to Martha; she was obviously well pleased with their results – her healthy baby boy was a perfect addition to their growing family. Martha would be sure to slip the coins into the hollow behind the loose dry mud along the edge of the fireplace where she kept the rest of their earnings. It was a slow process, but she was proud to have been able to put away a tidy sum over the years and Letitia was excited to be making her own contributions.

* * * *

Life went on, every day following well established patterns. Nothing ever seemed to change much. And actually there was some comfort in maintaining a routine. It might not be exciting but it wasn't frightening either; better to be a little bored than a lot scared all the time. One heard terrifying stories about some of the large plantations in the states farther south. Kentucky suited them just fine.

"I've been thinking, Momma. Tisha's been earnin' lots of money workin' with Binta and Martha at midwifin'. Do you think I could learn to do somethin' that I could earn money too?" Callie hoped her Mother would figure out something that wasn't too hard.

Polly regarded her daughter thoughtfully. "You're pretty handy, maybe you could learn to tat. I think Maggie over at the Barnes' farm might be willin' to teach you if Massa is willin' to let you go over there on your half day off. She learned fancy Irish lace patterns and some other styles. Tattin' would be a good skill to hire out; he might just allow it. "

* * * *

Letitia and Callie frequently talked about their plans for the future. Callie was learning to tat and hoped to be able to sell her fancy creations at the Mercantile in Clermont or even to the Mistresses of nearby farms.

Callie's Irish Lace Collar Pattern

"I don't want to stay in Kentucky forever. I got dreams. I'm savin' my money to buy my freedom someday."

Callie wasn't really surprised that Tisha had grand plans; she just didn't know how likely they were to actually come about.

"You could be right, but I'm not plannin' any such thing. I'm gonna find me a good-lookin' boy and get married. Then I'll just let him take care of me. I can use my tattin' money to buy nice clothes or maybe nice dishes for our cabin."

"Well, if it makes you happy, I guess you can do that if Massa lets you go. Better hope your good-lookin' boy has got plenty of money to trade for you goin' off with him."

* * * *

Sally's sudden appearance in their doorway early on a Sunday morning startled Binta and Martha. What in the world was she doing out in the near dawn twilight?

"Sorry to leave it so late, but I'm wonderin' if you want go to the prayer meetin' with me this mornin'. A good size group of us are gettin' together in the clearin' in the woods down the road in a bit. You two want to come along?"

"Well, I don't know. We need to finish our breakfast first." Binta murmured in reply. "What do you think, Martha?" she asked as she turned to look at her housemate.

"I've never been to a prayer meetin'. What'll we all be doin'?" Martha looked skeptical at this turn of events.

"First we sing some spirituals, church songs, you know. Then Luke's gonna be preachin' the Bible message this mornin'; he remembers almost the whole Bible. We'll have us a chat after, hear about the local goin's on. We can't stay long; some have got to get back to work and some of the massas don't like for us to meet in too big a group. I don't know what they think we're gonna do..." Sally's soft, perplexed voice trailed away.

Martha raised a knowing eyebrow at her housemate; they had heard lectures aplenty about expected proper behavior for slaves and the waiting punishment that would be meted out to anyone who broke the rules. "I suppose I can come see what it's all about this once. You gonna go, Binta?"

"I haven't been to a hallelujah meetin' in a long time. I reckon I could use some strong preachin' today. I'll come too."

Within a month they were regularly attending the little meeting in the woods each Sunday. Martha was impressed with the impassioned teaching and music that seemed to pour out of people's hearts. Sometimes the singing was joyous; sometimes it was low and sad. For the first time, she felt like she truly belonged. She was no longer a stranger in this strange land; she had her children and Jesus and Sunday sisters and brothers who cared about her.

Callie and Letitia attended the meetings too, but they weren't really interested in the praying and singing. They mostly whispered together about the young men from nearby farms and speculated about the most desirable qualities for them to possess as possible husbands. It was fun to natter together even though they weren't really serious. It never hurt to do a bit of planning for the future.

A short while later, during their evening visit, Callie was startled by an abrupt question from her best friend. What do you think about Momma gettin' religion?"

"I think she seems more peaceful like, don't you?" Callie sat thoughtfully for another moment. "I reckon it's been good for her."

"I suppose you're right. Maybe I should pay more attention on Sundays. I could use some of that peace in my heart too. Sometimes I get so tired of livin' in Kentucky. We don't have any say in where we go or what we do and I hate it somethin' fierce. I want to be free to decide for myself, don't you?"

"Now Tish, you know good and well I haven't got any big plans. I just want to be happy. I figure someday I'll find a good husband and not worry about anythin' else the rest of my life."

Chapter 13

How Time Flies

"Lord, Lord. Where has the time gone? It seems like just yesterday we were young and frisky. Now we're gettin' to be tired ole women, Martha." Binta stepped away from the wash tub to grab a rag and wipe the sweat from her forehead. Martha, who had been humming *There is a Balm in Gilead* under her breath, stood pondering the comment. She noticed Binta's hair was obviously getting much greyer and her face was developing wrinkles in spite of her slowly increasing weight. She was beginning to move slower too; it was hard for Martha to watch the beginning of the end. She wondered how old Binta was and how much longer she'd have her beloved friend. Like most slaves, they knew the general season they were born and how years had passed, but almost none knew their actual birth-date.

"Hooee, you got that right, though I'm not ready to be a granny yet even if you are five times already. Tish has grown up as tall as me. She's shapin' up to be a fine midwife what with you trainin' her and me helpin'. For sure we've birthed a passel of babies around this place and over to the neighbor farms. I'm just glad we haven't had any more of that cholera or typhus up here in Kentucky like's been hauntin' the lowlands in North

Carolina every year." Martha paused and looked out the doorway to where the grass was growing tall and green. It was so pretty now with the snow gone and the flowers poking up brightly colored heads everywhere.

So different it was here, so very different from home. Her memories of Shaki had faded badly. She didn't think so much about home any more, but she still missed her parents something fierce. She wondered whether her brothers were still alive and if they had wives and babies. She would never know, but it pleased her to imagine them happy and thriving in sunny Jamaica. After a moment, she shook her head slightly and turned back to stirring the boiling wash pot with the long poled paddle carved especially for the job.

"Tisha asked me yesterday how much I thought she'd have to save up from her midwifin' jobs to buy her freedom from Massa Bowman. She's had this on her mind since she got her first Christmas penny years back. I've decided I'm gonna ask the Massa what he thinks is a fair price. I sure do hope it isn't too much. What do you think, Binta?"

Binta stood staring at Martha with the most astonished look she'd ever seen. "Well, what?" She asked again.

Binta slowly closed her mouth and stood silently for a moment. "Oh Martha, I have to tell you I think that's the best idea I've heard in my life. I've got some money saved up and I'd be right pleased to offer it to help her be free. I'm way too old to dream of freedom any more, but Tisha's just right. When are you gonna talk to the Massa?"

Now it was Martha's turn to stare in surprise. Silent tears began to stream down her cheeks as she rushed to throw her arms around her housemate. "Binta, you're the best, kindest person I know. You're more like a sister now than ever before. I want to go right away, but the cowers have gotten hold of me again – I think I better wait a bit until I can face him calmly and sensibly. He might laugh in my face or chuck me right out the door."

She wiped her face on the hem of her apron as she went back to work. "I hear Massa William has started thinkin' about findin' another bride. So sad when his wife and baby child died last year. He really doesn't appear old enough to go havin' a family. Why, he hardly took to wearin' long britches but a couple of years back!" Martha smiled at that thought – maybe it was more than a couple...

Although, then again maybe, "I suppose it doesn't hurt any to look around and see which young'un might grow to be acceptable. Massa Kindred's brother has girls; maybe one of them would be alright for him. Fact is, isn't Sarah about Sally's age? She not too young and with her long red hair, she's pretty good lookin' when she's dressed in her Sunday go-to-meetin' clothes. Of course, more than 100 miles to Richmond is a bit far for courtin'."

"Now Martha, you're just bein' silly. William's plenty old enough to get a wife of his own without your advice or mine either. Let's get this washin' out on the line so we can get out of this hot ole shed; it feels like the gate to hell in here! I'm glad to turn this job over to Tabitha and Sally next month even if it's pretty near time to put out the new tobacco plants and start that endless hoein'. At least we'll be outdoors and it isn't hemp!

"I declare, Tabitha told such terrible stories about workin' in the hemp! I don't know how she could do all that bendin' and liftin' while totin' that baby boy. Of course, she was better off than the men who didn't get but 15 minutes for lunch and two cups of water every day. That Massa Prinslow sure was stingy. At least she got a break every day to sit and chop vegetables for the stew pot. And she got to use her sewin' skills almost every week on those men, cuttin' themselves with those machetes. Tobacco's hard but it's nothin' like hemp!" Binta took a deep breath and looked around the yard.

"Where's that girl of yours? I saw her and Callie headin' out to the south pretty near on to an hour back. We could use her help about now. Wringin' water out of these sheets is work for young arms and strong hands! And just lookee here," she exclaimed as she waved her hands at Martha. "I try to keep 'em out of the wash water, but it doesn't seem to help. That lye and ash soap has eaten holes in 'em again." She would need to slather them with soothing tallow tonight to avoid getting an infection in the sores.

This time Binta stuck her head out through the doorway. "Ah, here she comes." Letitia was striding quickly up the path toward home; her newly longer legs moving her along at a brisk pace. Binta admired her softer, older look before she hollered from the doorway, "Tish, get in here and help your momma and me."

"Yes'm Binta," Letitia called out as she broke into an even speedier trot. "I'll be right there just as soon as I hang this fresh lavender in our cabin. I want to get it started dryin' right away. Our supply's runnin' low and we need to make more candles."

"My my. That girl has grown up before I saw her doin' it. Martha, I tell you she makes me feel old as these here hills. I get tired just watchin' her. Won't be long and she'll be huntin' a husband for herself."

Fresh Lavender Ready to be Dried for Candles.

Martha nodded, then shook her head, as she replied, "You're right about her growin', Binta. I'm her Momma and I can't hardly believe it. But I don't think she'll look for any husband around here; she's gonna want a free man from up North. And I want you to know I went and talked to Massa Bowman about a cost for settin' Tisha free. I was surprised he set such a low price. With your savin's and mine and Tisha's, in another few years we'll have what we need. I tell you sister, she's gonna be so happy. I just hope I can hold myself together when it comes time for her to leave us."

Binta smiled compassionately at her housemate. "Well, it won't be any time soon, so you can rest easy for a goodly long while."

* * * *

The yearly rounds of chores helped break the monotony of long working hours. Planting and caring for vegetables and tobacco, and pruning the fruit trees in the Spring and Summer; harvesting food, gathering and storing bedding straw and moss, and butchering hogs in the Fall; sewing new household items and clothes, weaving replacement baskets, repairing and patching clothing and leather goods, and story-telling through the Winter. Time seemed to fly along faster and faster.

When Martha considered Letitia, head bent to her chores, she realized her baby girl was nearly grown up. Goodness gracious, she was already a teenager; it was past time to have "the talk" with her. She shouldn't put it off too much longer; Letitia was already attracting attention from the local boys and needed protection. Why was life so cruel sometimes? She would just have to do whatever she could for her beloved daughter.

Her older boys were already grown men. The thought made her feel ancient beyond her years. Still, she was pleased that they were all good-tempered, hard-working, and kind to her and others. She couldn't ask for more under any circumstances, even the ones she faced every day in Kentucky.

* * * *

"Come on Tish. Why don't you want to go for a walk?" William was doing his best to lure the girl away from her watchful mother, but she always seemed to have an excuse not to go along that made too darned much sense. He was pretty sure his father would be angry if she was wasting time, and going anywhere with him would certainly qualify. "Papa won't mind if you take a few minutes off. Really he won't."

Softly but insistently, Letitia spoke up, "Now Massa William, you know your papa doesn't want us bein' alone together. He's told me many a time to keep busy with my work and let you keep busy with yours. You know I've got to obey whatever the Massa says."

William scowled as he turned away. Wasn't she supposed to obey him too? He thought to himself how much he wished his Dad wasn't such a stickler about certain things. A romp in the hay wasn't a crime after all, and it had been a long time since his young bride had died in childbirth. Ah well, one of these days, one way or another, he'd find a way to get what he wanted.

In the meantime, maybe he'd just go over to see Franklin Barnes for an hour or so. His Daddy has several pretty young slave women who know how to treat a man…

Chapter 14

Into the Future

"Martha, I do declare, I never knew you were a seer. I can't believe William went all the way over to Richmond and got himself engaged to Miss Sarah. Wherever did you get such a notion? You were sure right enough about him."

Letitia eyed her mother curiously as Martha held out her skirt and dipped a tiny curtsey to Binta. It was awfully crowded in their little home, but love kept it cozy. Then Martha laughed as she grabbed her last son and hugged him to her knees, He lifted up his grinning face to peer at her. Job was a darling boy, nearly time for him to move to the men's sleeping quarters. She would like to have another girl, but babies were hard work on top of her advancing age and everything else she had to do. Maybe she should gather up a good supply of Queen Anne's Lace. Several parts of the plant were a help in preventing any more children coming along. It was a hard decision.

"Yep, I'm a seer of the future alright. Of course, it didn't hurt any that I saw William lookin' at Sarah every Sunday when they visited last summer like he thinks she's chocolate cake or mallow candy, somethin' soft and sweet."

"Where'd you see 'em? I know Massa Kindred didn't let her out of his sight if he could help it." Binta looked and sounded totally scandalized.

"Oh, they were down to the creek out by the church. I think they sneaked away from the picnic lunch on the lawn. Anyway, they were mostly behavin', just walkin' along, talkin' and makin' eyes at each other."

Bullitt County, Kentucky Country Church.

"Well, that's alright, I guess. I'm sure glad Massa Kindred didn't catch 'em though; he'd have given Young Massa a good lickin' with his ridin' crop if he saw 'em together without an attendant!"

"Hooee, you're right about that for sure! Well, it'll all be just fine now. They'll get married and find a place nearby, then everybody'll be happy. The Massa isn't so young anymore and he's gonna need all his boys to help with the farm here until Massa William gets his horse breedin' goin' good."

* * * *

Fall had arrived in the Kentucky hills; the leaves of the woods had quickly exchanged their summer multihued greens for yellow, orange, and red. Bears were out scavenging the bushes for berries, haunting the creeks for fish, raiding bees' nests, hunting the fat acorns that squirrels had been stashing away in singles and small caches, and digging out ant nests in search of as much rich food as possible; they would need extra weight to enable them to hibernate through the coming winter, especially the females that would be birthing new cubs in their secret dens. Good thing the males awoke periodically to rummage for food in the snow; they could be hunted if supplies in the larder were to get too low.

Most of the fruits grown in the Bowmans' small orchard of hardy apples (cider, pie, and eating varieties), pears, and plums were picked and safely stored away in baskets in the root cellar for later eating or drying, as were most of the vegetables.

Broccoli and late cabbage couldn't be kept for long but they lasted best in cool, moist conditions along with potatoes (unwashed and layered in straw) and mature green tomatoes which could be fried as is or kept to ripen a few at a time on the kitchen window ledge. Onions hung drying in long strings from rafters, but would be moved to straw-lined baskets next to the pumpkins and squash which liked cool, dry storage spots. Green beans and peas had been layered with salt in big crocks. They would be rinsed and rehydrated before going into soups and stews. A few items could stay out a bit longer as the ground got cooler but even those would need to be brought in before many more days passed.

Another impressive crop of tobacco had been cut, bundled, and dried. Six to eight weeks of air-curing the leaves produced the slightly sweet cigars prized by men everywhere. Once the leaves were ready, the bundles were piled into wagons and hauled away to be evaluated by the cigar experts at the market down in Louisville. It might not be edible, but it was right handy to be able to lay a bit of cash aside for unexpected emergencies and purchase of items that couldn't be grown at home or found in the nearby forests.

Tobacco Drying Shed on the Bowman Farm.

Most of the fully grown hogs had been butchered and hung in the smokehouse to cure. A few were soaking in an experimental heavy brine following the recipe being used in North Carolina. Everyone was worn to a frazzle after long hours, sunrise to sunset, laboring over the killing, gutting, scalding, skinning, and cutting. It was filthy, smelly work. Thank goodness it had to be done only once a year!

On the other hand, it was so nice to sit quietly in the cabin after a supper of fresh, battered and fried chitlin's and a potato baked in the ashes to the side of the fireplace. Fortunately, killing and scalding chickens and butchering the odd beef steer could be done as needed so they weren't such an exhausting chore.

All three types of carcasses were saved, the tougher cuts of meat and the bones, boiled in water and strained, then reduced to gelatin which was dried into pocket soup. Once the gelatinous chunks were wrapped in paper they could be used as stock for soups and camp fire meals when traveling.

Callie and Letitia continued to spend every free minute they could find together, chattering and laughing at shenanigans perpetrated by the older boys and the pratfalls of their little brothers. Plans for the future had been made and re-made a thousand times. Lately they'd begun to seriously discuss marriage possibilities among the young men on the various neighboring farms. They might not get a choice in the end, but it didn't hurt to develop a short list of preferences just in case.

Callie had already made up her mind that she wanted to find a way to latch onto the apprentice blacksmith over at the Pierces' place. She had gushed over Samuel until Tish didn't want to hear it again. "He's so-o-o handsome and strong! Can't you just imagine cuddlin' with him every night?" She hugged her arms and wiggled in a delighted shiver. "Mm, mm, mmmm!" She smacked her lips. "I mean, who wouldn't want to have that man for a husband?"

Tish had been forced to agree with her friend's assessment, but like her Mother had predicted, she was set on a man who was already free so they could raise a free family. Why bother considering some fellow who might be trapped in Kentucky forever or be sold away to South Carolina or Mississippi? Once her freedom fund was big enough she'd go somewhere safe and find a way to send for Momma.

Both days and nights were growing cooler in the shorter periods of Fall sunshine. Large carpets of moss had been peeled off dead trees and big rocks in the woods, then dried in great mounds. Over the next few days pits of dirt would be dug with the hoes so that mud could be created and mixed with moss to make chinking for the cabin walls to insulate against the cold winds that would begin to blow shortly. Winter would have to be endured in order to enjoy the Spring that would follow. And so it was.

* * * *

Spring had arrived in a rush of warm air, and myriads of flowers nodded their heads in the sun. Margaret Bowman hummed happily under her breath as she sashayed around the house, dreaming about the upcoming wedding more than she was actually getting any dusting done. She really couldn't entrust her fragile glass and china knick knacks to the hands of the house slaves. She didn't have to worry when she did it herself and once a week wasn't too difficult to handle.

"Why in the world am I thinking about *Turkey in the Straw*? That's hardly romantic music, though certainly not as silly as *Possum Up a Gum Tree*. They are both lively tunes, I must admit. I wonder what all the musicians will play at William's wedding reception. Oh, I can't wait to have another daughter-in-law! It took him long enough to settle on Sarah. I'm glad her family is staunch Presbyterian. It just seems right we all believe alike. The revival certainly brought us all together, though it seems as though we're all flying apart lately. All the children growing up and getting married. Families moving farther west.

"The folks up North have been butting their noses into our business with a vengeance; why can't they leave well enough alone? They want Southern trade crops but expect them to just appear out of thin air. Well, I guess those folks in Alabama and Georgia will have to settle it. I'm glad we're out of the way of all those arguments."

Margaret stopped fluttering her dust cloth to sit down on her best settee to contemplate the coming nuptials. There were dozens of beloved old hymns that might be played during the wedding itself, but none of them were suitable for dancing a nice cotillion or quadrille, and there was nothing wrong with a little modest dancing among family and friends…

A short while later, Abraham came in the front door calling loudly for his wife. "Where are you, Dearest? I'm starving for some good lunch. What're we having?"

He found Margaret sitting, staring blankly out the window, still day dreaming, having done nothing whatsoever toward planning his luncheon menu. It grieved him but he supposed that he must grant her a little grace since William's wedding weighed heavily upon her thoughts. Their kitchen girl Betsy could make him a fat sandwich of the roast pork left over from last night's supper. Yes, that would do just fine. And maybe a tall glass of fresh lemonade. Lemons cost dearly because they had to be hauled all the way from Florida, but they kept all winter and were so tasty with a spoonful of sugar. Oh yes, this was getting better all the time. He wouldn't scold dear Margaret; her burdens were already enough for her to manage.

As he made his way toward the kitchen he smiled at one of the barn cat's kittens playing football by himself under the dining room table with Margaret's pin cushion. He had never seen a soccer game, but he had heard it described once and the kitten's speed and striking accuracy certainly made him think of that midfielder his friend from London had told him about. Actually, the game had seemed a total waste of time and energy to him. Hastily, he called, "Betsy, get in here this instant."

Betsy hurried through the doorway as Mr. Bowman quickly hid the grin on his face, scooped up the rambunctious little ball of fuzz and held it out to her with a stern look in his eyes. "What's this fellow doing in the house? You know how Mrs. Bowman feels about animals wandering around on her clean floors."

Betsy reached out tentatively to take the kitten. "I'm so sorry Massa Bowman. He must have sneaked in while we were beatin' the carpets this mornin'."

"Well, get him back to his mother down at the barn and then get yourself back to the kitchen. I'm starving and I want a nice roast pork sandwich and a glass of cool lemonade. So, hurry up and don't waste a minute. I'll wait out on the front porch."

"Yessir, Massa Bowman. I'll have your lunch ready before you know it!" Betsy called back to him as she clutched the kitten to her chest to race outside and down the path to the barn.

* * * *

123

As the elder Bowmans stood on their front porch, surrounded by their younger though mostly grown children, waving good-bye to their oldest son and his new bride, Margaret smiled through her streaming tears. The buggy would take the couple safely to their new home in Elizabethtown before dark.

"What is it about a wedding that makes you women cry so? Aren't you happy William and Sarah are married at last?" Abraham was truly baffled. Even though he had seen this phenomenon many times, it didn't make much sense and none of his friends had ever been able to explain it to him.

"Don't be silly, dear husband, of course I'm overwhelmed with joy. All women cry at weddings; we can't help it. It's our tender sensibilities. Our babies are grown up and leaving home. It's a combination of happiness and sorrow, I guess. At least they won't be far away; we can see them often. I can't wait for grandchildren! I just hope Sarah can make it safely through motherhood."

Mr. Bowman patted his wife gently and escorted her back into their house where the slave women were quickly clearing up from the afternoon's festivities. Maybe he should suggest that she take a nap after their exciting day. Yes, maybe he should take one too; he was getting too old for all this uproar! Especially since

Martha had come to him yesterday to propose that he get Tisha's freedom papers written up. How on God's green earth had she managed to save up $200 in such a short time? On the other hand, having a little extra cash on hand wouldn't hurt his pocketbook any. Maybe he'd see about it later; she couldn't really have all that much hidden away. Then time just seemed to get away and his memory of his promise faded into nothingness.

Martha wondered whether the papers were ready, but it was too hard to bring up a touchy subject with the Massa, so she put off asking if it was time to pay. Letitia had no idea how much had been stowed away for her freedom project but assumed that it wasn't yet enough or Momma would have said something to her.

Chapter 15

Disaster Strikes

"Martha, I need to speak with you right now." Mr. Bowman looked harried as he rushed down the path to the east tobacco field where she and Tabitha were shearing the big leaves off the plants and stacking them for men to carry to the wagon parked at the edge of the field. They would then be hauled to the long shed where other men would be creating huge curing bundles which would hang loose for the next couple of months. Martha put the machete on the ground, hurried down the row to the end, and stood silently before her master. The cowers were back in full force! And how right they were...

"Sarah's getting close to her time and Mrs. Bowman is starting to worry about her. I want Letitia to go on down to William's place and be there when the baby arrives." Mr. Bowman looked abashed to even being saying such words about his daughter-in-law to another woman, and a slave woman at that. "She can stay there and help out; I really don't need three of you here."

Stricken to her heart, Martha looked up at him as the first tears welled in her eyes. "Oh no, Massa you can't be sendin' my gal away." She wailed in a shriek, sobbing wildly. "You promised she could buy her freedom and she's got the money you wanted. You can't send her away!"

"Now woman, don't you be taking on like this. It's not like I'm selling her to some plantation way off in Louisiana; I'm just loaning her for a while. She'll be down to the house in Elizabethtown. William and Sarah also bought a farm just a mile or so northwest of Thomas Lincoln's old place on Knob Creek. I know it seems like a long way, but it really isn't. I'm sure we can make arrangements for you to see her for a day or two a couple times a year when you aren't needed here."

Lord have mercy! A couple of times a YEAR? What was he thinking? Total panic flooded her heart.

"But Massa, you've already sold away my oldest boys. Please, please don't take my gal too." Martha tried to calculate how strongly he might react if she pressed her case too hard. She was glad he wasn't near as bad-tempered as some of the massas who struck their slaves without hesitation and got out the whip for even the slightest infraction of the rules.

"Now, Martha, you know the tobacco crop wasn't what it could've been last year; in fact, it's looking mighty peaked this year. The ground's getting thin I reckon. Anyway, I had to pay the bills. Mr. Connor at the

Mercantile needed a hand around the store and was willing to take Josiah in trade so I had to do it. You see him when you go to town for Mrs. Bowman, right? And when you're out at a birthing over near to Clermont?

"As for Thomas, well, I know he's a bit farther away and you haven't seen him since he left, but I hear he's doing well learning the blacksmith trade; he'll be very valuable once he's finished his apprenticeship." He thought his arguments were plenty reasonable. "So you just calm down." He put on his sternest face. "I've made my decision."

He studied her closely and came to another decision. "In fact, I'll even consider giving Tish her papers when the time comes. How does that sound?" Mr. Bowman used his best deal-making wheedle, hoping he wouldn't have to listen to any more weeping or complaining. He didn't like to use punishment on his slaves if he didn't have to – it just made them resentful, unfit to work as hard as they could, and slow-moving slaves were almost worthless. He needed every hand to be fit as a fiddle if he was to keep his tidy farm going. "You come to the house with the money and I'll get right over to town and have the papers drawn up all legal like."

Martha knew there was no changing his mind now that it was set. She stopped crying to consider his almost offer of freedom in exchange for this new shift in her daughter's life. It would certainly be worth whatever she had to do if she could secure that promise for Tish. Maybe she could come back after Missy Sarah's baby came. She would keep quiet about the deal she'd made until the papers were official.

"Alright Massa," she sniffled. "We'll do as you say." As he turned away and began hiking back to his house, she stood up straighter to watch him lumbering along, then scurried back down the row to resume her work. How wise she'd been to help train Letitia as a midwife when she'd asked to work with her and Binta; maybe Massa William would let her work out and earn more money for herself; she would need an income if she was to live on her own until she found a good man to marry. That would be sweeter than the jug of molasses they all shared on Christmas morning! Maybe this once everything would work out just fine for her family.

That night at supper she gave Letitia the news. "Now, I want your promise that you'll be careful, do a good job for Massa William so he'll tell Massa Bowman you're a worthy slave. And you find a church or at least a meetin' to attend soon as you can. Behave like a lady and you'll always be safe. The Lord'll be watchin' over you while you're gone just like your Momma has done every day since you were born. Remember your real name and our people. You've got no reason to be ashamed before anybody." She hesitated and then said again, "Just be careful."

Letitia almost asked about taking her money with her, but then decided it was probably safer staying here. She had been looking forward to being in charge of her own life, but evidently there still wasn't enough in the freedom fund. She was more than certain it would cost a small fortune to buy herself free. The value of a good slave had risen to unbelievable heights. Well, she'd keep doing what she could to help build up to the amount she needed.

"Yes, Momma. I'll remember every word you've told me." They reached out to hold each other in a tight embrace; Martha's head rested on Letitia's shoulder. Her baby was now a tall, slender young woman. There was nothing they could do about this separation; it would have to be endured. Silent tears rolled down Letitia's cheeks as she turned away to gather up what little she had to take with her. She wasn't too sure there was any way to be careful enough around Massa William. He and his friends had a bad reputation in the close-knit community of neighborhood slaves. He didn't always follow his Daddy's instructions as to proper behavior.

After the dishes were scrubbed and the floor swept, Tish grabbed her shawl and hurried out the door heading to Polly's cabin to tell Callie the latest news. The idea of leaving her best friend in the world was crushing. They wouldn't have long to visit and say their pitiful good-byes as Massa William was sure to turn up sooner rather than later.

In fact, William arrived the second day after with a small wagon to load up Tish, the supplies she would need to take care of Sarah, and her few belongings, which were folded into a small bundle and wrapped in three yards of soft tammy that his Mother was sending to be made into baby diapers. It was an exciting time but kind of scary too. Having been through it before, William wasn't anxious to face the possibility of loss again.

"Good-bye, Momma. Good-bye. Take care. I hope to see you again soon." Letitia watched over the wagon gate and waved as long as she could see the little scrap of cloth flapping at the end of Martha's fingers. Somehow she just didn't think this was going to work out as well as Momma was hoping. And it didn't.

Chapter 16

Bad News

"Come on, Tish; I haven't got time to waste while you dawdle along. I surely don't want Sarah wondering where you are and why you aren't up to the house taking care of Artemesia."

"I'm comin' along, Massa William. But, what if Arte starts cryin'? Missy's been puttin' up jam all week and she's tryin' to rest this afternoon. She's gonna be mad if I'm not there to soothe your little girl." Would he change his mind? Tish looked pathetic, begging to be released from this duty as strongly as she could without actually saying anything that might earn her a whipping. She decided to chance one more question, a really important one, "What's Missy gonna say if I get a baby from you?"

"For crying out loud. Get in this barn right this minute. Sarah hasn't let me near her since long before the baby was born and I've got needs to be satisfied. If you weren't dragging your feet you'd be back at the house already, certainly long before either of them wants you for anything."

He glanced apprehensively back toward the house then reached out to grab Tish's arm and throw her down on the small pile of hay just inside the door. His favorite stallion, startled at the sudden noise and motion, expressed his displeasure by rearing wildly and kicking out at the wall.

"You're alright, you fool horse. Just calm down and eat your oats. We'll be gone in a few minutes." He reached down, grabbing the hem of her dress to throw the skirt up over her face. Once he had hurriedly completed his "business" with Tish, he got up, refastened his pants, and stalked off without a second thought for the woman he left behind. His carelessness would cost him mightily!

Tish stayed in the barn for a few minutes to straighten the cast-off cotton dress Sarah had given to her. Letitia had outgrown all her own clothes, and motherhood had taken away Sarah's choice about wearing the dress herself. It had worked out well for both women, although Sarah wasn't particularly thrilled by her more matronly body. She wondered why William seemed to avoid her since Artemesia had arrived. On the other hand, she was too glad to be excused from his daily demands to broach the subject to him. She decided to let well enough alone.

Tish brushed hay off her clothing and picked it out of her hair—no point in rubbing William's activities in Sarah's face. It never served to upset the Massa's wife any more than it did to get him riled up. Best to just keep quiet and look innocent. Although, while Tish didn't yet know it, eventually there'd be no hiding what had been going on.

Oak Baby Cradle Hand Carved for William Bowman.

* * * *

Letitia continued doing every midwifing job she heard about even as her stomach grew larger. She wanted to make sure she collected as much money as possible while she could for earning freedom for herself and for the baby who would soon be arriving. There were several midwives in the Elizabethtown area and jobs weren't as frequent as they'd been at home. She kept her wages behind the loose board in the corner of her tiny room, which was actually a dressing room attached to Missy's bedroom. Please God, let it be enough!

* * * *

Lord have mercy! Letitia was nearly frantic with fear now that her monthlies were late again. What was she going to do? There was no way she could buy her own freedom and for a second baby in addition to her toddler. She wished desperately for time to go see Momma and get her advice and a supply of her Queen Anne's Lace. Nearly a year and a half had passed and she was still stuck in Elizabethtown trying to find excuses to not be alone with Massa William.

Now it was too late to get away. She really disliked having no say in what she did or where she went, but she especially hated having to submit to William's demands whenever he felt the mood. She wanted a loving husband, not "a roll in the hay" as William called it. She would ask Momma if they had saved enough to go to Massa Bowman. Maybe she and the babies could stay in Momma's cabin. Anything was better than staying here.

William thought long and hard about how to approach his father. Things certainly hadn't gone his way the last couple of years. Well, there was nothing for it; he had to go begging and that was all there was to it. In spite of that knowledge, he was still glad that it was more than a couple hours by buggy back to the old home farm. Maybe a brilliant idea would show itself before he actually arrived; one lived in hope when facing a father as furious as his was sure to be!

"Sorry Pa. I know you don't need any mixed breed children to feed and clothe on your farm, but Sarah's having a fit over Letitia's son being anywhere in her eyesight. I need you to take him off my hands or I'll never have any peace in my own home. Let Martha look out for him; she's his grandmother after all." William looked sheepishly at his Father and continued, "And I might as well confess now, there'll be another around about the New Year."

Mr. Bowman, looked at his son in horror. "What in the name of all that's holy were you thinking, son? I can't believe what you've done; you know I only loaned Tish to you for birthing, laundry, and child care, not to make a pack of yellow babies like all your friends have been doing. You've shamed your wife something awful when she's taken good care of you, your home, your child and with another on the way no less."

"Now Pa. You know Sarah's gotten bigger than a house this time around. I'm not so sure she won't have twins. I've gotta have some relief and I don't even want to think about what she'd say if I went to

136

Elizabethtown to the bawdy house. Besides, it's a total waste of money when Tish is right to hand. Come on, Pa. Help me out here. I'll even owe you a future favor," he offered, hoping to break down his father's resistance to the idea of having mulattos on his farm.

"Alright, but two is all I'm taking on and I'm getting rid of them just as soon as they'll bring a decent price. You figure out some other way of getting around your wife next time! Now go say hello to your Mother."

He scowled heavily at his son's departing back, then muttered darkly, "And I know just how to fix your wagon. Since Martha says she's got the money, I'm going to write up Tish's papers tomorrow as soon as you head home and once I give them to Judge Campion; he'll make sure they're followed to the letter." He waited until William left for home the next day before seeking out Martha to get the $200 they had agreed on. Dang nab it, he should have asked for more, but he had never gone back on a deal and he wouldn't do it now.

A month later he had made the trip to Clermont twice to see the Judge. His copy of Letitia's manumission paper was safely hidden in his desk along with his last will and testament, and Abraham felt more at ease.

That winter was rough on everyone, especially Margaret. Her health had been precarious for months. That deep cough had hung on so long, he was sure she was on her deathbed.

* * * *

It turned out she wasn't, but she was never really well again either. She spent a lot of time sitting on the porch in her favorite rocking chair, a shawl around her shoulders and a blanket on her lap even on warm Spring days. He hated seeing her suffering. It was almost a relief when she finally took to her bed and breathed her last in early Summer.

God knows he missed her terribly and felt certain he wouldn't be long in joining her. Maybe he should consider what needed to be done in the near future. If he got rid of most of the slaves it would cut his costs greatly. His crop yields had been dropping steadily; thank goodness his children were grown and out on their own. The whole problem made him feel old and sad. Then again, it was the way of life. Who was he to question the Lord's plans? Best to trust and just get on with whatever he could still do.

The market for slaves being sent farther south was still running hot. It didn't take long for Abraham to find buyers for most of the slaves he still owned. It was hard to watch them trudging off down the road, but it was time for him to give up active farming. Just keeping a little garden going, a couple of cows, a few chickens, and a sow would be enough work to watch over.

Chapter 17

Worse News

Winter in the Kentucky Hills.

It was snowing and getting dark when Letitia hurried through the door of Martha's cabin. "Happy Christmas, Momma. I'm so glad to see you again. Massa William says that since it's snowing again, he'll be here in three days with the wagon to see his Daddy and take me back. What's happening with ole Massa Bowman? Massa William's been looking awful worried lately. He and Missy have been saying his Daddy's feeling right poorly. I surely do hope it isn't anything serious." Letitia took off her bonnet and shook the snow off her cape as she bent down to kiss Martha on the cheek. "You're looking mighty spry yourself. I was awful sorry to hear that Binta went on to Glory before harvest. She was a dear woman and you all must miss her something fierce!"

As Martha started to get up from her chair, Letitia waved her back saying, "No, no, Momma. You rest and I'll get the kettle on. You want some bread and jam with your tea?" She added a couple of dippers of water to the black cast iron kettle and slid it onto the hook. Then she stirred up the coals and added another chunk of wood before swiveling the kettle over the flames in the fireplace. Her movements were smooth with both natural grace and long experience.

"Yeah, that sounds right temptin'. Happy Christmas to you too, Daughter. Lord of mercy, but you're just like your Momma, chatterin' away like a chipmunk. Although, I hear Missy's still makin' you talk fancy like her.

"Let's see. First, you've heard right. Massa Bowman's sinkin' like a stone. He's so far gone Betsy told me he's been lettin' Rex sleep in a box behind the kitchen stove. Can you imagine havin' that big ole stinky dog in the house? Why the Missus must surely be turnin' in her grave over that. Anyway, I suspect he won't live to see his comin' grandchild. Hooee, things'll be changin' around here again for sure. How's Miss Arte? I reckon she must be half grown by now. And how're those twins doin'? They must be comin' on for three years if my figurin' is right."

Letitia continued to bustle around the tiny room, setting two cups, a spoon, and a tiny dish of jam on the table; when the tea water boiled, she'd get a loaf of bread out of the storage box and cut off a slice to share. She took a long, narrow wrapped package out of her carpet bag and set it next to one of the cups. "I brought you a little present Momma. I hope you like it."

"Humpf. I suppose I'll like most anythin' you bring me." She scooted her chair over to the table and took up the package. "Let's just see." As she worked the paper loose, her favorite scent came wafting up. "Oh my, lookee here. I declare, these candles smell like heaven. Letitia, you're the best daughter I know. I sure wish I had a gift for you!" She reached out to pat her daughter's hand.

"Oh Momma, I'm just glad you like them. I'm sorry to hear Massa Bowman hasn't been well. Of course, he's getting up in years now so we can't expect him to live forever. I know what you mean about Missus Bowman having a fit whenever one of her children brought some animal into the house; how she carried on about the dirt and fleas and who knew what else they had all over themselves! I wonder if that's how Massa William got the idea to let Prince have a box behind the kitchen

142

stove in Elizabethtown this winter. Well, I guess the Massa can do as he wants now. What do you think's gonna happen to all the folks here? I know Massa William's been hinting around that he might sell up and move away once his Daddy's gone. I just can't imagine not living close to you all.

"I'm so sorry for carrying on when you've got the latest news on your mind. Yes, Miss Sarah is still saying I've got to talk like a lady so she can understand what I say, at least so long as I'm living down in Elizabethtown. You've never seen such tiny babies as Nancy Jane and Tabitha were the day they were born. They were so puny we weren't sure they could live, but they're just fine as frog hairs now. And Miss Arte, well, you're right – she's getting taller by the day; she's gonna pass right on by her Momma before long.

"Where's Tabitha? Where're the boys? Have you talked with Callie lately? I hear she and Samuel got married last year and she's gone to living with him over on the Pierce farm; can't believe the Massa let her go. Does she have a baby yet? I miss her something fierce! I wish she still lived close enough to see her while I'm back, but there's not enough time and the weather's too nasty. Tell me everything I've missed out on this past year!"

"Well, child." Martha looked away and hesitated far too long before going on, "I reckon you've got to hear it sometime, may as well be now. Massa Bowman sold everybody away except me and Betsy up at the big house. He says he can't take care of so many folks any more. We've come into hard times here since the Missus passed on. I'm just hopin' and prayin' Massa remembers his promise to me before he sent you off to Massa William."

"Oh Momma." Letitia had turned ghostly pale and looked ready to faint. "That's the worst news I've heard since I left here. Is everyone really gone? Tabitha? Polly? Does Callie know? Are my boys gone too? Where are they? I haven't seen them since Massa William sent them here after they were weaned. Are they close by?" Letitia began to weep so hard she could scarcely breathe. She sat on the floor to keep from collapsing. Martha watched and waited in silent sympathy. After several minutes she reached out to pat her daughter on the back. So much suffering for one so young. It seemed to happen all too often in Kentucky.

Finally she said softly, "All of them are gone. I'm right sorry to see you so sad. Guess I've had enough time to get used to the idea by now. Massa sent your boys off in the same slave train with Sally and my Job so she could watch over them until they got down to Alabama or wherever it was they were headed."

Letitia sniffed noisily and wiped her eyes then hugged her Mother tightly about her boney shoulders. "It hurts so bad, Momma, but I know we all are gonna be alright. We've still got each other. What kind of promise did Massa Bowman make to you? I never heard tell of any promise!" She sat close and held Martha's hand as if she might somehow disappear from in front of her eyes.

"I'm sorry I brought it up; I don't want to get your hopes high if he's forgotten. We just have to wait until he's gone to find out what he's done or not done." She sat in silence for a minute, wishing that she had asked him about Letitia's papers before he got so sickly.

"Let's just sit here by the fire; my ole bones have been achin' somethin' fierce this Winter. Samuel paid a hefty sum to get Callie loose from Massa Bowman. She's free but Samuel isn't so they're still livin' at the Pierces' farm. She's earnin' good money from her fancy hand work so maybe someday... I can tell you stories about home if I can remember any and we can talk about the ole times when this was a happy place. Besides, what's all this about maybe movin' away? Massa William isn't really gonna leave Kentucky?"

"I honestly don't know Momma. There's lots of talk of new land that came available in Missouri back a year or so. Missy can't be traveling with the new baby near to coming, but in the next year or two I do think Massa

William is gonna hie off farther west even if it is still Indian country. He's been wanting to go looking over the horizon for quite a while. I expect he'll get his wish once he's able to sell the farm and the house in Elizabethtown. Race horses are so popular now that farm is worth a small fortune and their beautiful house in town too. Shouldn't take very long at all to find buyers when the time comes."

"Well, I sure do hope he isn't expectin' me to hie off with you all. I'm too old and set in my ways for such nonsense."

"Now Momma, you surely aren't expecting me to go alone, are you? Course, maybe whoever buys Massa Bowman's farm would let us stay in this little cabin of yours. We got the money we saved, and I've got more at Massa William's. We could grow vegetables and do our midwifing for cash money. What do you think of that idea?"

Martha carefully avoided answering Tish's question about the money. All she knew for sure was that she had given it to the Massa and not seen it again. "Humpf. Sure does sound mighty appealin' to these ole ears. Rather stay than traipse off over hill and dale. Reckon we just have to wait and see what comes."

"Oh, Momma. You always say that. But then, of course, it's always true."

The next three days passed all too quickly. The ride south was cold in the icy wind, but at least they had blankets and the wagon to make it easier.

Chapter 18

New Life

Letitia knelt hunched over on the porch, rocking and sobbing so hard she could barely breathe. News just seemed to go from bad to worse these days. William stood just outside his front door watching her somberly. He hated having to give bad news and this was the worst. He remembered his mother's long illness and subsequent death; it had been hard on the entire family.

"I'm right sorry about your Momma, Letitia." William looked and sounded truly distressed. "She wasn't so old, but I guess the cold just got in her lungs and carried her away. Strange how Daddy died before her by only a couple weeks; we were expecting him to pass on but not Martha. Good thing Betsy was able to get word to Mr. Barnes or we might not have heard about him until just now. I'm sure glad we had that little break in the weather so we could all go back to the old farm for the funeral."

Letitia got to her feet, swaying as she wiped her face on her apron and thinking about having to attend another funeral so soon. Oh Momma, how will I live without you too? It was too much to bear! She needed her Sunday sisters. They would know what to do.

They would help her survive this horrible blow. But she couldn't just walk away; she would have to wait until later.

William continued his train of thought, "Ole Judge Campion sent word that he'll be down to settle Daddy's estate as soon as the road dries out a bit, maybe even next month if the good weather holds."

Well, that only meant the move to Missouri was coming sooner than she had hoped. After the burial, she would visit her Mother's cabin to search for the money she'd left behind. What if she couldn't find it? She should have asked Momma where it was when she'd gone to visit at Christmas. Then again, what if it still wasn't enough. With Massa Bowman gone, she'd have to strike a bargain with Massa William – no way to know if he'd be willing to let her go.

Although, what difference did it make anyway? Momma was gone, along with every other member of her family. She was just as alone as Momma had been when she arrived from Africa. People said, "The Lord works in mysterious ways." She sure couldn't find any argument with that. She would have to wait and see what was coming.

Letitia was quite surprised when Sarah and William decided that the whole family would go to the old farm with her to say good-bye to Martha. "It's only right," Sarah explained to her. "Your Momma was a hard-working, loyal slave and a big help to Daddy Bowman. We must pay our respects."

Letitia just hoped it didn't mean she'd be prevented from scouring the cabin for her freedom fund. And it didn't. However, in spite of her diligent hunt there was no large stash of money to be found, only a few paper bills and a pile of coins under a loose brick in the hearth, which Tish wrapped in a scrap of rag and put in her pocket. What could Momma have done with the money? They'd had quite a collection – it just didn't make sense.

* * * *

Two weeks later, the Judge was sitting at the desk facing William in the big wing-back chair by the window in the library. "So, that's the long and the short of it." He swept a hand through his long white hair as he finished speaking and stood to his feet. William jumped up and met him as he came forward. At his advanced age, he had to look up when handing the will and deed to the old farm over to William. "I sure hope your good wife gets to feeling better soon."

William snorted, but nodded in agreement. His son was barely a month old. Near as he could figure it'd be another month before Sarah was ready to take on anything but caring for the baby even though the girls were delighted to hold him and rock him in the cradle when he got fussy. He'd have time to get Daddy's farm sold, parcel out the bequests to his brothers and sisters, and start getting his own house in order.

"I thank you kindly, Judge," William nodded his head as they shook hands, "for making that long trip down from Clermont. I know that's a rough ride on horseback. Are you going to spend the night in Elizabethtown before you head back? You're sure welcome to stay with us if you like."

"I won't put you to any trouble, what with having a newborn." He didn't say it aloud, but he thought, 'I may be old but I have more sense than that.' "I'll just stay in town at the Hospitality House so I can get an early start in the morning. I don't trust the weather this time of year and surely don't want to get caught in a late snowstorm."

As the Judge turned to leave through the sitting room, he passed the other paper to Letitia who stood silently in the doorway in stunned amazement.

Why hadn't Momma told her that Massa Bowman had agreed to set her free? She had assumed that the money was lost, but Momma had used their money and bought her freedom after all; their plan had worked! She stared down at the writing she couldn't read.

"I'm free?" She whispered to herself. "I'm really free? It says that? Oh. Oh my, this must be the promise Massa Bowman made to Momma all those years back." No, she thought to herself. He's not my massa anymore; he's just plain ole Mr. Bowman. She folded the paper carefully and slipped it into her apron pocket. She'd have to tuck it in with her money to keep it safe; this was now her most precious possession!

She used to imagine one day when she would escape like Papa had done, but fear of patrollers had started the cowers that bound her feet like ropes. She had dreamed of living free with her own family in Ohio or somewhere else up North, but that dream had faded after she had been sent to Massa William in Elizabethtown. Now it had actually happened. She could go wherever she wanted.

William and Sarah had discussed heading to Missouri next year. They had planned to take her along to help care for baby Will. Now, she could go or stay as she wanted. Since she was no longer a slave, she could ask for a servant's wages and be respected as a free woman. "Hm-m-m," she murmured as she considered the idea. "There's nothing to keep me here. I can choose for myself. I think... I think it would be good for me to go out West." For the first time in a long while, she had hope of finding real happiness.

She felt different. She was her own woman. She felt brave. She would take this opportunity to step into the new life that awaited her.

#######

To learn more about Letitia read:

A Light in the Wilderness, by Jane Kirkpatrick. (Grand Rapids: Revell, 2014), 324 pp.

Access:

Friends of Letitia Carson, on Facebook, by Dr. Bob Zybach, Janet Meranda, and Jane Kirkpatrick. Source of hundreds of documents, maps, and photos.

More Reading:

Olaudah Equiano, "The Interesting Narrative of the Life of Olaudah Equiano, or Gustavus Vassa, the African," in Henry Louis Gates, ed. *The Classic Slave Narratives* (New York: Mentor, 1987), pp. 32-37.

Joseph Hawkins, *A History of a Voyage to the Coast of Africa, and Travels into the Interior of that Country* (London: F. Cass, 1970 reprint of 1797 ed.), pp. 140–149.

James C. Klotter and Freda C. Klotter. *A Concise History of Kentucky* (University Press of Kentucky, 2008), 238 pp.

Marion B. Lucas. *A History of Blacks in Kentucky From Slavery to Segregation, 1760-1891* The Kentucky Historical Society, 2003), 430 pp.

Johann David Schoepf. "2.6 A Slave Auction at Wilmington." *Travels in the Confederation (1782-1784)*. Translated and edited by Alfred L. Morrison (Philadelphia: William J. Campbell, 1911)

Barbara J. Starmans. "The Journals of Thomas Thistlewood, Sugar and Slavery in 18th Century Jamaica." www.thesocialhistorian.com based on Thistlewood Archive, Beinecke Rare Book & Manuscript Library, Yale University.

Kentucky Slave Narratives: A Folk History, The Federal Writers' Project 1936-1938. Applewood Books, Bedford, MA and Library of Congress. Available on-line or recently published new edition (Native American Book Publishers, 2007).

GLOSSARY

Banshee – Irish name for the "fairy woman" who heralds death with moaning, shrieking, and wailing.

Beehive Oven – A small free-standing dome-shaped brick chamber for baking.

Cat o' nine Tails – A 30-inch, multi-braid leather whip.

Chitterlings – Pronounced chitlins. Pig intestine stuffed with ground pork, a sausage.

Ehefrau – Wife (German).

Gool – The original English name for the children's game of *Tag*.

Grossvater – Grandfather (German).

Hoe – A griddle for cooking on open fire.

Jump the Broom – Colloquial phrase for the informal marriage ceremony between slaves.

Klungel – Clan (German).

Mamba – A large venomous snake species which inhabits parts of Sub-Saharan Africa.

Mush – Corn meal porridge.

Opa – Grampa (German).

Pika – A small mammal related to hares and rabbits that looks similar to a large mouse without a tail.

Porridge – Boiled ground grains such as corn, oats, rice, or wheat.

Pottage – Grain meal-thickened soup.

Puncheon -- A split log or heavy slab of timber with one face smoothed, used for flooring or other construction.

Running – Slaves who escaped were said to have run.

Settee – A small sofa with seating for two.

Shoat – A newly weaned young pig.

Slops – A gooey stew of fruit and vegetable materials unfit for human consumption, made for pigs.

Sohne – Sons (German).

Tammy – A mixed-fiber wool and cotton fabric.

Tick – A thin pallet or mattress which rests on the floor.

AUTHOR'S ACKNOWLEDGEMENTS

My deepest thanks to my dear friend and award-winning author, Jane Kirkpatrick, whose writing skill and style have long held my heart captive. How I admire her in every way.

My thanks are first for taking Letitia into her life four years ago and devoting herself to getting Letitia's name and story told to thousands through her historical novel, *A Light in the Wilderness*. Second, thanks also for allowing me to be a resource to help ensure the greatest possible accuracy in that telling. Finally, thanks for encouraging me to move beyond my fears to write the prequel to her story through *Freedom's Light*. May your readers enjoy this novel as much as I've always enjoyed yours.

Thanks also to Anna Austin who didn't hesitate to volunteer to illustrate this book. She turned random historical photos into material-specific sketches that are perfect.

Another thank you goes to my graduate school research partner, Dr. Bob Zybach, who suggested I write Letitia's story for a young adult audience. I hope you like the way it turned out.

My final thanks go to our friends David and Rebecca Prinslow. When I told them I was writing this book, Rebecca said "Put David in the story. Make him a bad guy; he'd like that." So I did.

AUTHOR'S NOTES

While *Freedom's Light* contains much more fiction than fact about Letitia's early history, it's as accurate as the facts known to me at this time.

1. The Muslims invaded southern Spain and took control in the 700s. The Spanish Castiles spent hundreds of years at war to retake the peninsula. King Ferdinand of Aragon and Queen Isabella of Castile jointly commissioned Columbus in 1462 to find a western route to Asia and Africa to bypass the Portuguese stranglehold on trade. Then the two married each other in 1469. The Inquisition was established to create a Christian population; Jewish and Muslim citizens were ejected in 1492 and 1502, respectively.

2. Farm horses began arriving in the colonies in the 1600s from England where fast horses were already being bred from Thoroughbreds and Arabians imported from northern Africa. Heavier standard horses and draft breeds were favored for farming in the early United States. However, as racing horses became more popular in midcoast states such as Maryland, New York and Virginia; smaller, faster horses became wildly popular in Kentucky. Lexington (Keeneland and The Red Mile) became the racing capital of the United States and remains so to this day although there are other world-famous

159

tracks (Churchill Downs in Louisville, Turfway in Florence, and Ellis Park in Henderson) also in Kentucky.

3. The working of the sugar-rum-slave trade of the 1700s and 1800s is well documented. Don José Barbosa did indeed sail his slaver *Feloz* around that trade triangle in the early 1800s, so I borrowed them for this story.

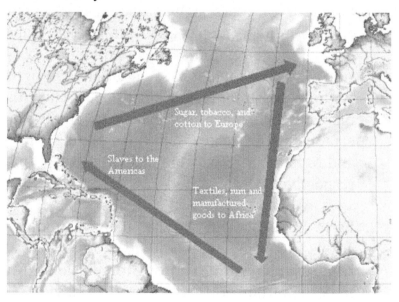

Chapter 4, Section 6: The Triangular Trade. *Boundless U.S. History*. Boundless, 09/20/16. See https://www.boundless. com/u-s-history/textbooks/boundless-u-s-history-textbook/

4. Savanna-la-Mar had a popular southwestern Jamaica slave market, smaller and less dangerous than the one in the capital city, Kingston. Thomas Thistle-

wood lived in Savanna beginning May 4, 1750, worked first as a sugar plantation overseer, and later managed his own market farm, growing flowers, livestock, and vegetables. His many slaves were frequently rented to neighboring sugar plantations, thus ensuring a healthy income for their master.

5. Slavery was a part of North Carolina history from its first settlement by Europeans in the early 1700s all the way through the American Civil War. The first 1000 slaves were resident by 1705. After the primitive road system had been improved, coastal Wilmington had a thriving slave market, sending slaves both farther south and farther west.

6. Corn became popular with colonial cooks after Native Americans introduced the crop to them in the 1600s. In the late 1700s colonial wheat was being exported to England and Europe, so Indian corn, or maize, was adapted for bread, which the English would not eat, considering it pig food. Poor colonists and slaves survived mostly on heavy unleavened fried cornbread, which didn't look very appealing (because the kernels were yellow, blue, red, purple) but tasted okay. The English thought of corn as strictly inedible hog fodder and laughed at the colonists who ate it. See *Memoir of a Revolutionary Soldier: The Narrative of Joseph Plumb Martin*, Joseph Plumb Martin (Reprinted Glazier Masters & Co, Hallowell, Maine 1830 edition), 176 pp. or listen to James Townsend on at https://www.youtube.com/watch?v=tVuWJ54CjpE.

This recipe is from Amelia Simmons, 1796, as presented by James Townsend.

Common Bread
1 C milk scalded
3 Tbsp butter
1 Tbsp molasses
Pinch of salt
Stir well.
Add:
3 C corn meal
.5 C wheat flour if desired
Mix well. Form dough into flattened cake. Fry on both sides, or bake at 375° for a half hour.

7. There were several egg preservation methods used in the colonies and continued into early U.S. history. The most successful were storage in jugs of lime water or covered in tallow in small wooden casks, both keeping eggs fresh for many months when needed. However, tallow was more popular because it didn't change the taste of the eggs, although lime water had fewer failures over time.

8. Ginger Switchel

1 Gal fresh water
1 ½ C molasses
⅓ C apple cider vinegar
1 Tbsp fresh ground ginger root

Mix well, store in covered crock and keep cool. High potassium revitalizing drink.

See http://www.almanac.com/blog/cooking/cooking/switchel-or-haymakers-punch-recipe.

9. Jim Beam® bourbon style corn whiskey was first produced by Jacob Böhm in 1795 after his family had moved from Germany to the United States. Eight generations of their family continued their tradition of fine bourbon. The distillery is located in Clermont, Kentucky and is a popular tourist destination today.

10. Letitia was born in Kentucky in the early 1800s, although she herself claimed two different birth years in two later Oregon census rolls and a third birth year is computed by subtracting her age from her death date as recorded on her tombstone. Kentucky, unfortunately seems to have no record to help clear up the confusion. We don't know Letitia's parentage, but her skin color was described as being "coal black." This coloring is found among tribes located near the Equator across Africa, which is how I came to choose the Yoruba for Letitia's heritage, since they also live close to the west coast and were taken as slaves, sometimes by the Fula.

11. Abraham Lincoln was born in 1809 on Sinking Spring Farm near Hodgenville, Kentucky, southeast of Elizabethtown. The family later moved 8 miles

northeast to a farm on Knob Creek. His family then travelled on to Indiana in 1816 and finally in 1830 to Illinois.

12. The Prinzlau family is believed to have come from Poland. Leonard Cagle's grandfather immigrated from Obermehlingen, Germany and Leonard's two oldest sons were named Lindsey and Henry. The LaForce family emigrated from France; they were taken from Kentucky to Canada as POWs during the Revolutionary War. At that time, René, the oldest son, was already serving with the colonial army as did Elizabeth Cagle's father, Drury Smith. Elizabeth Smith Cagle did not get another daughter until 1828, two years before Willis was born. The LaForce and Cagle families did move to Carthage, Missouri and were joined through marriage during the Civil War. The Cagle family owned a dairy and horse-drawn milk delivery service there. My maternal grandfather, Thomas Jewel Cagle, was born in Carthage.

13. Letitia left Kentucky sometime prior to 1845 and moved to Missouri. That was the year she left Missouri with David Carson heading west on the Oregon Trail. Whether or not she had any children before joining forces with David is unknown as is whether or not she was a slave or a free woman in Missouri. It is still my hope that more details of her life before 1845 will be discovered in the future.

APPENDIX

MAPS

Current Countries of Africa.

Modern Sierra Leone. Freetown was established by the British in 1792 in order to re-settle approximately 1,200 Loyalists of African heritage from America, Canada, and England following the American Revolution. The settlement became a refuge for thousands of Africans who were liberated from slave ships following the abolition of slavery in Britain in 1808.

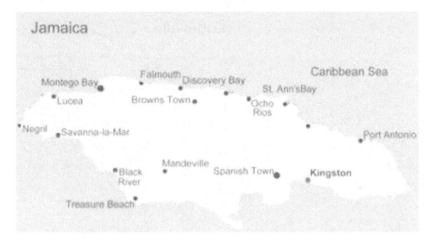

Kingston, on the southeast coast, is on the seventh largest natural harbor in the world. The city was established in 1692 after a massive earthquake destroyed Port Royal. It became the capital city in 1872. Savanna-la-Mar was founded in the 1700s on the southwest coast but completely destroyed by a hurricane in 1780. After it was rebuilt it went on to become a major slave market until slavery was abolished in 1839.

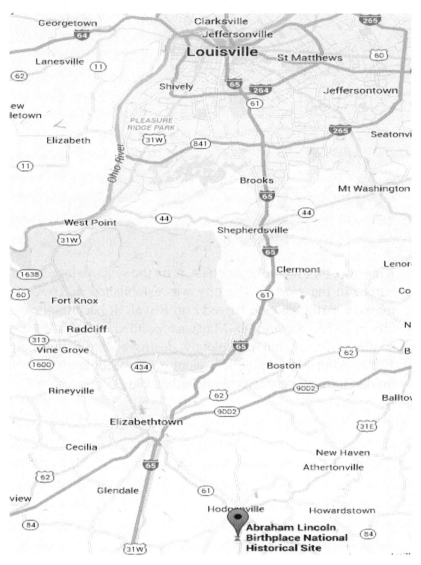

Louisville to Clermont is about 25 miles. Clermont to Elizabethtown is also approximately 25 miles. Hodgenville, Elizabethtown, and Knob Creek, Kentucky are within 15 miles of each other.

Made in the USA
Middletown, DE
14 August 2021

45318703R00096